T0155152

FLYNN
AND
MIRANDA

Your Right to Remain Silent

A HISTORICAL NOVEL BY

JOSEPH B WALLENSTEIN

Cover Design: Ed Bishop

Published by:
Trine Day LLC
PO Box 577
Walterville, OR 97489
1-800-556-2012
www.TrineDay.com
trineday@icloud.com

The following manuscript is a work of historical fiction. Names have been changed, time lines altered and creative license taken. It is based on a true and accurate retelling of a story found in the transcript of a recorded conversation between attorney John J. Flynn and the author.

Library of Congress Control Number: 2020947090

Wallenstein, Joseph B. Flynn and Miranda: Your Right to Remain. Silent—1st ed.
p. cm.

Epub (ISBN-13) 978-1-63424-311-7
Mobi (ISBN-13) 978-1-63424-312-4
TradePaper (ISBN-13) 978-1-63424-310-0
 1. Fiction 2. Historical 3. General 4.Miranda, Ernesto -- Trials, litigation, etc. 5. Right to counsel -- United States. 6. Self-incrimination -- United States. 7. Confession (Law) -- United States. 8. Police questioning -- United States. I. Joseph B. Wallenstein II. Title

FIRST EDITION
10 9 8 7 6 5 4 3 2 1

Distribution to the Trade by:
Independent Publishers Group (IPG)
814 North Franklin Street
Chicago, Illinois 60610
312.337.0747
www.ipgbook.com

TABLE OF CONTENTS

PREFACE

NOT JUST A LEGAL DECISION ...
A PIECE OF YOUR LIFE

The book *Flynn & Miranda* tells the story of two men from opposite ends of the human social spectrum who came together in one blazing moment of legal history. That moment changed their lives and the lives of all Americans.

Ernesto Miranda was an anonymous street tough, whose name became synonymous with the greatest legal decision of the twentieth century. But it was Attorney John Flynn, a larger than life, highly successful and controversial attorney, who did the heavy lifting.

Look at *American Heritage* magazine's list of ten people who have changed your life of whom you've never heard and you will find attorney John J. Flynn. He was well-known to local Phoenix Arizona area residents. He had defended more than one hundred death penalty cases, and had the highest exoneration rate of any local attorney. He was constantly embroiled in highly controversial cases, a thorn in the side of the Arizona power structure, and the brunt of bitter rebukes from the *Arizona Republic.*

John Flynn was the man they loved to hate. His life was as turbulent as those of the clients he represented. Married five times with two sets of children, he gambled wildly, and was a lousy businessman who got stiffed by most of his clients. He was also a serial adulterer, and was dragged before the Arizona Bar Association, accused of drug possession, and consorting with a known prostitute. He fought the charges, was exonerated and kept right on practicing law.

Flynn was very savvy.

When Ernesto Miranda's case was dangled before his law firm, Flynn knew it was a once in a lifetime opportunity. Certain to be unpopular, sure to be controversial, he took it because it was the right thing to do ... and it was a possible opportunity to plead before the United States Supreme Court.

Later, when Miranda was tried a second time for rape and kidnapping by the state of Arizona – upset that its dirty laundry had been aired on the public stage – Flynn stepped up again.

1

Flynn's involvement in Miranda's retrial was the final straw for the Phoenix Police Department. Flynn was attacked by three off duty officers and had to fight for his life, but he never abandoned Miranda.

Flynn & Miranda grew from a one-of-a-kind opportunity to meet, question and record my time with John Flynn. The conversation took place at his home four months prior to his sudden passing. He told me: "I have been asked about the case a thousand times. You are the only guy who has ever asked me about the *price paid* by me and my family"

This is that story…

PROLOGUE

THE TURBULENT SIXTIES

Women burnt their bras. Men burnt their draft cards. "Hippies" and police clashed from Greenwich Village to the Haight-Ashbury. In law enforcement, the inherently-tainted "confession" was known as the primary tool of police work.

Today, thanks to movies and television, most Americans know that a policeman placing a suspect under arrest is obliged to inform that person of his or her "rights.

> *You have the right to remain silent. Anything you say can and will be used against you in a court of law. You have the right to have an attorney present during questioning. If you cannot afford an attorney, one will be provided you free of charge.*

But what most Americans do not know is as recently as 1962 it was possible to be taken from your home, accused of a crime, denied legal counsel and kept in prolonged custody subject to the coercive will of the police, without law enforcement or the courts doing anything wrong.

That egregious conduct was simply permissible then.

Given the overwhelming advantage enjoyed by the police, one would think that law enforcement in those days was a snap. Isolate a suspect, coerce a confession and march into court.

Ironically, the most common criminal defense was: "Sure my client confessed. They scared the living daylights out of him." Or: "They beat him into admitting something he didn't do," and blind the jury to all other facts in the case. So pervasive was that defense that hundreds of patently guilty felons went free.

However, something remarkable was happening in 1962.

A supposedly conservative United States Supreme Court, known as "the Warren Court," for its Chief Justice, the former Governor of California, Earl Warren, was turning out to be surprisingly liberal. By the winter of 1962, the Warren Court had heard *Mapp v. Ohio*, *Gideon*, and *Escobedo*, all cases dealing with fourth, fifth, and sixth amendment issues.

In some legal circles it was believed that the time was right for a case that would pull together and define, for all time, the compendium of individual rights extended to citizens on the federal level: i.e. The Bill of Rights.

Into that moment of historic legal possibility stepped two unlikely combatants, Ernesto Miranda, street criminal and John J. Flynn, Attorney at Law.

What made the Miranda case even more improbable was the well from which it sprang.

In 1962 Phoenix, Arizona was the home of the growing conservative movement and its leader Barry, "Extremism-in-the-Pursuit-of-Liberty-is-No-Vice," Goldwater. Some of its citizens were Mormon. Phoenix and Tucson, only sixty miles to the south, attracted many elderly retirees who craved the dry desert, climate. The newspapers were conservative. The police were conservative.

And, most of all, the courts were conservative.

In addition, in 1962, there was no American Civil Liberties Union (ACLU) in Phoenix. They relied on "Correspondent Attorneys," lawyers who took "significant-issue" clients on a case-by-case basis.

Miranda's case, at first look, was no different than a hundred others. Accused of kidnapping and rape, he was arrested, isolated, denied legal assistance and tricked by the police into bearing witness against himself. His trial lasted only two days. He was convicted and sentenced to thirty years in prison.

And he would have served every minute of it had his case not caught the eye of former Assistant District Attorney, Robert Corcoran.

Corcoran, who then worked as a defense attorney, had come to view the law through the frightened eyes of his poor and uneducated clients. Miranda, an indigent defendant, unknowledgeable about his rights as a citizen, had been removed from his home and subjected to prolonged interrogation by two large men with guns on their hips.

But Corcoran felt his status as an officer of the court at the time of the original trial precluded his participation in any appeal. He needed to attract the attention of an outside attorney.

And not just any attorney. He would require someone special!

Corcoran was sure the Miranda case would be unpopular. Corcoran had an extensive network of relationships throughout the local power structure. He realized the appeal, if successful, would create a rift within the close-knit legal and social structure of the city. The case was certain to create the impression that police methodology was on trial. Indeed, the entire city and its way of life would be held up to public scrutiny.

Therefore, you would have had to be a little arrogant or extremely crazy to handle the task.

You would have had to be ... Attorney, John J. Flynn.

CHAPTER ONE

It Never Rains In The Valley Of The Sun

Phoenix, Arizona, January 1976

It never rains in the Valley of the Sun.

At least that was what the plaque imbedded in the floor of the Phoenix International Airport said.

But the rain bore down in rippling sheets the night John Flynn flew his single engine Cessna back from his fishing trip to Kalkeetna, Alaska. It had been an exhausting twenty-four-hour flight with two refueling stops.

Flynn had needed to get away. He was Phoenix, Arizona's most successful defense attorney and yet, his last client, Manuel Silvas, a Mexican laborer, had been put to death in the Arizona gas chamber, a barbaric method of execution destined to be banned.

The gifted attorney had fought, using all his considerable skills, to get the state to spare the man's life. After many months, the appeals had run out. Even a last-minute plea to the Governor had been denied.

An hour before the scheduled execution, John Flynn sat with the condemned for the last time. His heart was so heavy he could barely speak.

So, his client spoke, "Don't feel bad, John … you done good."

An hour later, the man was dead and John Flynn was on his way to Alaska.

On his way back, Flynn rented a four-wheel drive jeep and drove up into the snow-covered slopes of Brundage Mountain. The mountain had been named after his great grandfather, the first man to bring sheep to northern Idaho. The lush verdant fields were perfect for grazing.

Flynn had spent his summers there as a youth. There was an old homestead, long since abandoned, that still remained. It stood tumbled down in weather-ravaged disrepair. There were corrals as well.

Flynn's grandfather had been business partners with a Basque shepherd named Chevarier. Brundage was cattle country and new-comers were met with aggression and hostility.

Flynn's father had once been arrested for cattle rustling. He was eventually exonerated and went on to become an attorney. But Flynn and Chevarier survived, often through bloody range wars. It was a part of family history seldom discussed.

To John Flynn, Brundage Mountain was a haven, his safe place away from the greater, darker world. He had retreated to the grounds of his youth after the agonizing failure to save the life of Manuel Silva.

An hour from McCall, he fished along the Salmon River above Riggans in west central Idaho. He struggled with his emotions and, begged his god for forgiveness.

Born in 1925, John Flynn was seventeen when he lied about his age and enlisted in the Marines. He saw combat in the Pacific theater, on the black sands of Iwo Jima and in the monsoons of Luzon in 1945. War, as it did to all who experienced it, brought horrific haunting images. Flynn witnessed a fellow marine sliced in half by airborne corrugated metal swirled into a projectile by monsoon winds.

On Iwo Jima he was standing talking to a fellow marine when a bullet went entirely through the man's head. Flynn fireman-carried his wounded comrade three miles back to bivouac. Running across the ruts, over rocks and through the brambles, he was buffeted by the deep rumble of exploding artillery. Bullets whizzed by his head.

For Flynn it was the embodiment of the Marine Corps creed of: "Leave no man behind."

The end of the war brought him little peace. At night the images of his fallen comrades violated the dark and lingered like specters on his weary shoulders. He struggled to adjust to civilian life, but post combat adrenalin addiction was slow to abate. He enrolled mid-term in the University of Arizona, attended three years and got his law degree. As the decade of the fifties dawned, Flynn became a member of the Maricopa County District Attorney's office.

When things were slow, his cravings for action drove him to strap on a Colt .45 and go looking for bad guys himself. "A clean up the town sort of thing," he would later say.

Those actions brought him into contact with a young, up and coming member of the Phoenix police department named Carroll Cooley. Cooley was a good man whose hefty

PD. PHOENIX, ARIZ.
APPO NTED   PHOTO
4·28 ·58   413   10· 9 ·63

size belied his gentle nature. Cooley came to think of Flynn as "one of us." They became friends and eventually fishing buddies.

In the years between 1946 and 1952, the eternally restless Flynn hunted for emeralds in Ecuador, became a marathon gambler in Las Vegas and purchased a pecan farm in Gilbert, Arizona. He was bad at the first two and deep in debt because of the third.

Eventually, out of financial necessity, he had turned his energy to becoming a defense attorney and started his own law firm.

In 1952, wealthy Arizona socialite Evelyn Smith was kidnapped and held for ransom. Mrs. Smith was a member of a prominent, if controversial, family that owned Smith Pipe and Steel. Her husband, Herbert Smith, delivered the ransom money in a briefcase to a remote part of the Superstition Mountains. Upon receipt of the money, Mrs. Smith was released.

An itinerant named Danny Marsin was arrested and charged with the crime.

Danny Marsin engaged the services of fledgling local defense attorney John J. Flynn. Marsin was acquitted when, in his summation to the jury, Flynn railed against injustice and the belief the prosecution had failed to prove their case beyond a reasonable doubt.

Danny Marsin was eternally grateful to John Flynn and proved it by stiffing his attorney on his fees.

For Flynn, payment came in another form. The publicity surrounding the case sent his reputation soaring.

In 1959, he was approached and asked to join the largest, most prestigious law firm in Phoenix, Lewis and Roca.

By the time the name "Miranda" appeared on the horizon, Flynn was struggling through his fifth marriage and attempting to raise his second set of children.

* * *

CHAPTER TWO

COMING HOME

Phoenix, Arizona, 1976

In the Phoenix airport, John Flynn's family waited for him at the exit railing. The usual throng of exiting passengers had thinned as the hour grew late.

Annie, John Junior, and Michael. As they always did when they saw their father, the children ran to him, arms raised. First to reach him was Annie. She threw her arms around him, to say that she had reached him first. It was pure affection.

John Junior got to him second. He emulated his sister. The oldest boy, Michael, approached more slowly. He hugged his father and kissed him on the cheek.

Only Camille, his wife, hung back. She knew why he had gone. She would give him the time and space he needed to regain his equilibrium.

Camille was not his first wife, but she was the mother of his children.

Camille had grown up in Tucson. In her twenties, she had been first runner-up in the "Arizona pretty" pageant. Even now, after having birthed three children, she continued to possess a cowgirl's figure.

Camille had crystal clear brown eyes and chestnut hair cut short. She bore a tan, the result of hours spent in the sun.

Horseback riding was her preference – but she played country club golf. It was an admittedly incongruous pastime for her but one in which she felt compelled to participate as the wife of a successful, high profile attorney.

Michael, the oldest child, bore a striking resemblance to his mother. Tall and slender with dark eyes and smooth skin. He too seemed to have been blessed with a perpetual tan. Shy by nature he possessed an athletic ease. They shared Camille's love of horses. Michael took gentle care of their stallions, Chester and Apollo, aware of his mother's affection for the animals.

Michael cherished the times he and his mother would ride their horses into hills above Carefree, a northern Phoenix suburb. Together they searched the red-rocked caves and appreciated the ancient drawings that adorned the walls.

Michael was the perfect combination of his father's ruggedness and his mother's good looks.

Annie, the baby, was the most like her father, full of energy and exuberance. She skipped everywhere she went. Even at an early age it was obvious she would grow to be a beauty. Annie wore her jet-black hair in a tightly wound pony-tail that swished like a horse swatting a fly. Everyone said she was the spitting image of her father.

John Junior, they called him "Scottie," struggled against the perpetual paunch of pre-adolescence. Not exceedingly athletic, he participated in every team sport in a desperate attempt to garner his father's attention.

Scottie did not particularly resemble either one of his parents, a reality that fostered the whispered malicious observation that he looked more like their mailman. It was an inappropriate joke that caused Camille to bristle.

After all, it was not she for whom fidelity, or the lack thereof, was an issue.

At the car, Camille handed John the keys. He would drive and regain some sense of control. They rode in silence. Before long Annie and John Junior fell asleep resting against one another.

Michael stared vacantly out the window.

Camille placed her hand on John's leg, her quiet way of saying, "I am here for you when you are ready."

After a few minutes, John reached over and turned on the radio. He lowered it so as not to wake the children. It was the top of the hour news:

> **Phoenix, Arizona:** *Ernesto Miranda, the man for whom the momentous States Supreme Court decision was named was stabbed tonight in a bar room altercation. He had been selling autographed "Miranda warning" cards as souvenirs. When police caught the suspects, they did not have their own cards and used one found on Miranda to warn the assailants of their rights; Rights won for them in the name of the man they had just killed. Local Attorney John J. Flynn argued the controversial case before the United States Supreme Court.*

Flynn turned off the radio.

Camille could see the effect the news had on him. He gripped the steering wheel a little tighter. His gaze had become a stare.

Camille withdrew her hand from his leg and said softly, "I'm sorry."

11

They pulled into the driveway of their Gilbert, Arizona home. He had still not spoken.

Camille offered, "You go on up. I'll see that the kids get to bed."

John went upstairs and got into his pajamas. He brushed his teeth and prepared for bed. But instead of getting under the covers, he stood staring out the window.

He lit a cigarette. It was the last one of the second pack he had smoked that day.

Camille undressed silently and slid into bed. She did not disturb her husband.

Miranda's death had hit him hard.

John Flynn had many an emotional mile to go that night.

As he stood at the window, prior events flooded his memory.

* * *

CHAPTER THREE

TREADAWAY

Phoenix, Arizona, 1963

Daniel Treadaway was running through the woods.

Branches scratched his face. Fatigue slowed his legs.

It was something out of a bad prison movie.

Treadaway was running for his life. He could hear the hunting dogs howling as they closed on him. They had tracked his scent. Men's voices were raised in excitement.

They were gaining on him.

Running, short of breath, legs aching in agony, Daniel Treadaway collapsed and waited for the inevitable.

The men descended on him more viciously than the dogs. The dogs merely surrounded him and snarled. The men punched and kicked him. One produced a rope and draped it around his neck.

For one terrifying moment, Treadaway believed they intended to lynch him right then and there.

But his fate was not to die at the hands of an angry mob. He would be brought to trial, convicted and sentenced to die in the Arizona gas chamber for the sixth of six homosexual rape murders of young boys.

John Flynn had gotten Treadaway's initial conviction overturned. He was defending Treadaway at his second trial.

Still standing staring out the bedroom window, Flynn thought about how and when he had first gotten involved with Daniel Treadaway.

It was the evening Don Boles' divorce was finally final. Flynn had been his attorney. Boles had been an investigative reporter for the *Arizona Republic*.

It was not kind of the case that would normally be represented by John Flynn. But he and Boles were friends from the day, as a young prosecutor, Flynn had brought allegations of income tax evasion against the *Arizona Republic*. It was Arizona's leading newspaper and enjoyed enormous political clout.

It had not been much of a celebration, just some champagne in the law offices.

As day turned to dusk, the participants began to drift off.

Flynn would just clean up a little and head for home.

But as he slid into his suit jacket and looked towards the door, an elderly man was standing there. He held his hat in his hands, "Please, Mister Flynn. A moment of your time … I beg you."

Curious about what the man could want, Flynn invited him in.

Almost immediately, the man began to weep, "My son, Mister Flynn. He will die. They will kill him."

A little taken aback, Flynn asked the man to sit.

It was the father of Daniel Treadaway. Treadaway was schedule to die in less than a month. His father was desperate to find someone who could file an appeal in his case.

Flynn listened to everything the man had to say … and agreed to take the case.

Flynn was neither intimidated by, nor repelled by, controversy. In fact, he thrived on it.

He was "the Man they loved to Hate."

He had challenged the state's most influential newspaper and won. He had handled the biggest headline-grabbing cases and prevailed.

Judges listened carefully to what the "Master Summation Man" had to say. But Treadaway?

There had been five previous rape-murders of young boys in the Phoenix area. All five had been sodomized and strangled. Vigilante groups had been roaming the Phoenix area night after night. The case was personal. Every parent felt the gut-wrenching agony of the victim's demise.

Treadaway had been found guilty and sentenced to be executed. The case had many flaws.

So many, in fact that Flynn had succeeded in getting the state to grant a retrial.

The case had been all over the front pages. Treadaway had been convicted because his palm print had been found and identified on the window frame outside the sixth victim's bedroom and a pubic hair found on the boy's buttocks.

It was widely believed that Treadaway, a known burglar, was also homosexual.

Flynn's strategy had been to challenge the authenticity of the medical examiner's "expert" witness. The man had stated, under oath, that the pubic hair found on the dead boy's buttocks belonged to Daniel Treadaway, "beyond a shadow of a doubt."

There had been something else. Treadaway was a slender sparrow of a man.

He looked more like a wounded bird than a malicious predator. It was difficult for Flynn to reconcile the image with the allegations.

Flynn had forced himself to become his own "expert" on pubic hair. And in order to do that he had to read many books on the subject. He was relentless in his pursuit of information and laser-focused on becoming his own specialist. Night-after-night, day-after-day, he trudged valiantly through the research.

What he discovered was, in those days, the best anyone could say about pubic hair was "it might be from a human." It was virtually impossible to definitively say it was human or unique to one individual.

And, if that was true … what was the point of any medical examiner's testimony on the subject?

• • •

CHAPTER FOUR

THE RETRIAL OF
DANIEL TREADAWAY

Phoenix, Arizona, 1963

The retrial of Daniel Treadaway had begun. On the morning of the third day, Flynn and the prosecutors gathered beneath a framed picture of John F. Kennedy in the chambers of Judge Claymore. Flynn was anxious to get the medical examiner on the witness stand.

The prosecutor, impeccably dressed, was about to have his day. He would preen, pronounce and perform for the jury.

But he was up against "the Jack-of-Hearts," John Flynn. Flynn was pacing like a caged tiger between his empty chair and the Judge's window. It might have been the judge's space, but the room belonged to Flynn. The prosecutor and the judge watched Flynn's calculated restlessness like spectators at a tennis match.

The judge finally broke the hypnotic performance, "John, I'm concerned, you're taking too big a risk with your client's future."

Flynn shrugged off the judge's concern: "Second degree murder. Life without parole. Doesn't sound that good to me."

"You're taking an awful gamble," Judge Claymore replied.

The prosecutor spoke up, "It'll sound great when this jury finds him guilty. He'll be straight on his way back to the gas chamber."

The judge agreed, "Tom's right. And this time, there'll be no room for appeal. I've been very careful."

The prosecutor took his cue from the Judge. "We've got his palm print on the window outside the kid's bedroom. We know he's a burglar. We've got a hair sample. Treadaway must be a homosexual ... it's a pubic hair."

Flynn stopped pacing. The two men stared at him in hopeful anticipation. But Flynn began to pace again, forcing them to start scanning back and forth again.

"Jesus, John" the Judge blurted in frustration, "The sixth of six homosexual murders of little boys. People been roaming the streets of Phoenix for months looking for the perpetrator."

The prosecutor tried to seize the moment. "And when I put the griev-ing mother on the stand, they might as well drop the pellets right there in the court.

"What do you say, John" The Judge pleaded?" Let's save the taxpayers of Maricopa County some time and money."

Flynn looked as if he were contemplating their suggestion, but: "I want to hear from the Medical Examiner."

The judge let out an audible sigh.

The prosecutor tried to bridge the silence gap, "Christ, we got his con-fession."

Flynn was not impressed by the prosecutor's assertion. "I'll bet you have his confession. You've got a tight case, right?"

Flynn started for the door out of the Judge's chambers.

"Air-tight," pronounced the prosecutor just a little too quickly.

The Judge and the prosecutor watched as Flynn walked from the office closing the door behind him.

For the first time that day, the prosecutor felt a small bead of sweat roll down his side.

* * *

CHAPTER FIVE

REMEMBERING THE DAY
MIRANDA DIED

Phoenix, Arizona, 1976

Midnight came and went and still Flynn stood and stared. He broke the cellophane on his third pack of cigarettes. He tried to imagine how the day of Miranda's violent demise had unfolded.

January 31, 1976 had broken grey and gloomy. Ground-fog cloaked the Maricopa County Courthouse in mist and mystery.

One man, Ernesto Miranda, stocky, with jet black hair, paced relentlessly back and forth. Miranda, was in his twenties and had an athlete's physique. He carried himself with the swagger of a street fighter. He was there to sell his "Miranda" cards as souvenirs to the tourists and the curious. Three dollars unsigned, five if he personally autographed it.

The occasional hippy in bell-bottom jeans and scraggily hair wandered through the mist like an apparition.

Rod Stewart's "Tonight's the Night" blared from an anonymous car radio.

At first, the pickings were slim. But, as the morning wore on and the ground mist lifted, business picked up. Around eleven the sun erased the last vestiges of the cloud-cover. By that time, Miranda had amassed the small fortune of forty dollars.

He ambled around the corner to his favorite cantina, the Amapola Café.

The Amapola Café was a small bar, unremarkable in every way. Sawdust on the floor and sunlight through the door combined to form a gritty haze. A picture of President Gerald R. Ford hung proudly on the wall above the bar. Eddie Palmieri's "Unfinished Masterpiece" belched from the juke box.

The man was handsome, in a slightly dangerous way, was her first thought about him. A clean shirt, new haircut, he might have been attractive.

Mary Lou had worked the Amapola for six years. She disliked both the job and the clientele. But the Amapola was only six city blocks from where she lived. She had endured long-term genetic arthritis. It weakened her knees and swelled her ankles. The long hours on her feet made a bad condition worse. But its close proximity to home made the employment

possible. So, she endured the rude customers, the low wages and the genial depression that hung over the cantina like a shroud.

Miranda seated himself at a table along the back wall, his face fading into the shadows.

Mary Lou was an experienced waitress and barkeep. She could sense trouble before it developed. As she watched the sullen stranger, her internal clock of impending strife began to tick.

She remembered he had been there before. She recalled that he would drink beers and many of them. She did not wait for him to summon her. She popped the top off a bottle and brought it to his table.

Two men entered the bar. The first one, Fernando Zamorra-Rodriguez, was thirty. He was the bigger and more imposing of the two.

The second man, Eduardo Esquillez, was twenty-eight. He was slender and more athletic looking. As they reached the table, the older man spoke, "Ey Hombre, quierres jugar cartes?"

For a moment they stared, taking the visual measure of one another. But Miranda was not intimidated, "Si."

The men sat opposite him. One produced a deck of cards.

Mary Lou retreated to the safety of the bar. But she would keep a wary eye on the men and the table.

Furtive glances amongst the customers paid tribute to the level of tension in the Amapola that had risen dramatically.

By four o'clock that afternoon, the clutter of bottles on the table mirrored the time on the wall clock.

Mary Lou noticed Fernando pass a card to Eduardo. A sense of dread rolled through her stomach.

The men placed their cards on the table. Miranda had two kings and two jacks. Eduardo had three queens.

In spite of her wary premonition, the explosion startled Mary Lou. Miranda threw up the table and attacked the two men. Glasses broke and blood spilled. Mary Lou ducked down behind the bar and dialed the police: "Come. Come now. They're fighting. Please. Come now."

When she stood back up Fernando was on the floor and Eduardo was trying to struggle back up to his feet. Feeling momentarily vindicated, Miranda walked towards the bathroom to wash the blood off his hands.

Fernando got up and stumbled over to Eduardo. He lifted him back up to his feet. Fernando reached into his back pocket and withdrew a lettuce knife. He handed it to Eduardo. "Finish it," he directed calmly.

Miranda emerged from the men's room.

Eduardo rushed at him. He thrust his lettuce knife into Miranda's chest. Miranda staggered back. Eduardo thrust again, this time into his abdomen. Miranda bellowed like a wounded animal. Driven by pain and adrenalin, he leapt forward trying to get his hands around Eduardo's throat.

Eduardo continued to flail away at Miranda.

Mary Lou screamed into the phone, "It's terrible. It's terrible. They're killing him. Come now!"

* * *

CHAPTER SIX

UNIDENTIFIABLE PUBIC HAIR

In Judge Claymore's courtroom, Daniel Treadaway sat at the defense table, appearing frail and frightened. His eyelids fluttered uncontrollably as he tried to bear the weight of the world into which he had been thrust.

The room reeked of perspiration and anxiety.

Two burly detectives, Carroll Cooley and Wilfred Young sat in the first row. They glared hatefully at Treadaway. Treadaway scrunched down in his chair. He wilted beneath the withering stares of his arresting officers.

The Medical Examiner was on the stand and John Flynn was questioning him.

"Doctor Ellis, you've examined the defendant's hands?"

Doctor Ellis nodded. "Yes. He appears to have a particular skin disorder. It's got a long and complicated name but basically the skin on his palms completely peels every six weeks or so."

Flynn started to pace. The judge, the prosecutor, the jury and all the spectators were forced to move their heads in lock-step with him.

After a thoughtful moment, Flynn broke the hypnotic silence, "So... you can't say beyond a shadow of a doubt that the palm print was made at any one precise moment."

Again, Doctor Ellis agreed, "That's correct."

Flynn stopped pacing. He turned to the witness as if perplexed by his answer. "Doctor, you've heard expert testimony that the pubic hair found on the child's buttocks belonged to the defendant, Daniel Treadaway."

"Yes."

"Do you agree?"

"No," Dr. Ellis responded without hesitation.

Flynn feigned surprise, "No?" he asked loud enough to be heard in the adjacent courtroom.

"No. You can weigh a pubic hair. You can scale it, measure it, treat it chemically and the best you can say is it might be from a human."

Flynn stopped pacing abruptly as if shocked by the answer. "Might be human? Not male or female? Not from any one particular individual?"

Doctor Ellis shook his head emphatically, "No sir."

Judge Claymore's eyes involuntarily shifted toward the prosecutor.

• • •

CHAPTER SEVEN

COPS WITHOUT CARDS

Police Officer, Doren Buhlheiser was only a block from the Amapola when the call came in. He activated his patrol car's lights and sirens and sped toward the cafe. He misjudged his approach and bounced his police car onto the sidewalk.

Two chicanos were just running out and slammed into the incoming patrol car. The force knocked them back into the cantina.

Buhlheiser and his partner jumped out. But Fernando and Eduardo were not about to go peacefully.

The younger office, Jerry Rivers, tried to grab Eduardo in a headlock. Buhlheiser wrenched Fernando's arm behind him in order to cuff him.

Eduardo slithered out of the headlock and pushed Rivers away. Rivers got just enough of Eduardo's shirt to keep him from getting away. Eduardo slipped and fell. He pulled Rivers to the floor with him. The two men wrestled around in the sawdust.

Buhlheiser managed to pin Fernando up against the wall but needed both hands to restrain him. He could not reach his own handcuffs.

Mary Lou had come out from behind the bar carrying several dish rags. She stuffed them under Miranda's shirt in an attempt to staunch the bleeding. She tried to concentrate amidst the chaos. She looked up. "He's … he's … dying."

Buhlhesier made the mistake of turning his head toward Mary Lou. "Get a god damn ambulance in here," he bellowed.

The momentary distraction allowed Fernando to push back into Buhlheiser, pushing him away. Fernando turned and tried to reach for Buhlheiser's gun.

"No, you don't, you son-of-a-bitch." Buhlheiser lunged at Fernando and drove both of them onto and across a table. More glasses shattered, more wooden tables splintered.

Rivers had pinned Eduardo, face down, onto the floor. He had succeeded in cuffing one wrist but was struggling to secure the other. In frustration, he drove Eduardo's face into the floor over and over again. "Quit strugglin', goddamn it."

A foot away, Buhlhesier finally had Fernando pinned. The older officer had placed his forearm across Fernando's neck as a restraint He had the suspect pinned to the floor.

Fernando's face was turning red as he struggled to breathe.

Rivers finally managed to cuff Eduardo.

Buhlhesier searched his own pockets for an admonition card. Chest heaving from exertion, temper shortening from frustration, he turned towards his partner. "Read'em."

Rivers was still dealing with Eduardo who continued to struggle.

"I can't get to my card," he yelled to his partner.

"Habla ingles?" Buhlhesier asked Fernando angrily.

"No," was the surly reply.

Buhlhesier hauled Fernando to his feet and shook him. "Ta hell with all of it.... Let's go, asshole,"

* * *

CHAPTER EIGHT

EXONERATION

In Judge Claymore's courtroom, Flynn was speeding toward culmination, "Doctor, you examined the body of the deceased?"

"Yes," Doctor Ellis affirmed.

"What is your finding?"

"The boy had pneumonia," Doctor Ellis responded quickly without equivocation.

Flynn hesitated dramatically.

"Pneumonia? They say strangled. Any rope marks?" Flynn wanted to know.

"No," replied the Medical Examiner, shaking his head.

"Bruises from hands?"

"No."

"Then how did this boy suffocate?"

Doctor Ellis cleared his throat for dramatic effect. "He choked on his own phlegm," he stated purposefully.

Flynn let that settle over the courtroom. He could hear an almost imperceptible murmur.

"Explain," the defense attorney prodded.

Doctor Ellis paused in order to get his points straight. "His lungs produced an elevated amount of fluid. It rose to his throat. It cut off his breathing."

Like a matador going in for the kill, Flynn turned his back on the witness to look at the jury, "Doctor Ellis, is this a case of murder?"

The silence in the courtroom had turned deafening.

Doctor Ellis shifted his body so he faced the jury, "No."

The room erupted into chaos. Shouts of outrage and screams of disappointment rang out.

Judge Claymore rapped his gavel repeatedly in an attempt to restore order, but he could not quell the bedlam.

Flynn's work was done there. As Flynn walked back to the defense table, he momentarily locked eyes with Cooley and Young.

This time, they were staring hatefully at him.

With the case essentially shredded, Treadaway was exonerated; at least, for the murder of the sixth young boy.

Outside in the hallway, Flynn waited for the elevator. Exiting spectators murmered their dissatisfaction with the verdict. Passersby glared angrily at the successful attorney.

Treadaway and his mother and father came out of the courtroom.

"God bless you, Mister Flynn," his father spoke. "God bless you."

Flynn addressed Daniel, "Daniel, get as far away from this town as you can and stay away."

Daniel Treadaway kept his gaze to the floor but nodded in the affirmative.

"God bless you, Mister Flynn," came the mocking voices.

Carroll Cooley and Wilfred Young had exited the courtroom and were approaching the elevators.

The doors opened allowing the Treadaways a graceful and timely exit.

Flynn waited for the two officers to reach him. It had been a stressful trial and he was in no mood to be needled by the police. Irked, he responded, "Damn right, Carroll. If you're going to charge someone with murder, at least make sure the crime really happened."

"Oh, we're sure it happened," Cooley responded.

"That and five others," Wilfred Young chimed in.

Flynn was not about to back down, "You think he committed those other crimes, you should have charged him with them."

Cooley stepped in front of Young confronting Flynn, "We had his palm print on the window."

Flynn was unmoved, "From six weeks earlier. All it proved was that he'd gone there to rob it."

Young was clearly agitated, "You got all the answers."

Flynn turned toward Young, "Tommy Burton died because his mother was drunk and asleep on the living room couch while he choked on his own spit."

Cooley was also badly frustrated, "So, the people just go back to living in fear."

"Hope not," Flynn replied. "Now, maybe your department will work on the five killings that really did happen."

The doors to the first elevator, the one farthest from them, opened. Flynn moved towards it. Cooley continued to harangue him, "That's good, John. The next time a child is raped and murdered in this town, we'll bring the parents by your house and you can explain it to them."

The elevator doors closed granting Flynn temporary respite from their outrage.

* * *

CHAPTER NINE

Verge Of Anxiety Attack

Flynn had to maneuver around the road construction. He flinched to a sudden halt as a pair of long-haired hippies glided in front of him as if they were the planet's sole occupants.

Ever since the bus strike and the road work, the city was growing more difficult. It had grown in size. They were adding another terminal in Sky harbor airport. Margaret Hance had been elected mayor the year before.

"Funny," Flynn mused. "Through her entire Republican election campaign, she had been billed as "the first woman Mayor of an American City."

It was sad how few people ever challenged that assertion.

Flynn knew that the first female mayor had been elected in Seattle. Her name was Bertha Knight Landes. Involuntarily humming, he was starting to feel the giddy mood swings that had always been his bellwether of post-trial decompression.

The traffic had thinned by the time Flynn guided his late model Chevy into the driveway of an upscale suburban Phoenix home. It was a home befitting a successful Arizona defense attorney.

Inside the front door, Camille waited for him, martini-in-hand, "Congratulations," she greeted, handing him his victory reward.

"You've heard," he asked, searching her face for some sign of support.

"It was on the news," she said stone-faced.

"Son-of-a-bitch, it feels good," Flynn admitted.

But Camille needed her husband back into the real life of his family, "I found cigarettes in Michael's room."

Flynn was slow to react.

All Camille's frustration bubbled out, "Annie might fail math. My car broke down on the freeway and the dog is sick."

It was Camille's way of reacquainting her husband with the world beyond the cocoon of his concentration.

Her salvo felt like an assault. It instantly irritated him.

"Give me some time, Camille," he barked.

He downed the martini in one gulp and handed the empty glass back to her. He moved past her towards his office.

Camille, now irritated and annoyed, retreated quietly to the kitchen.

In his home office, Flynn plopped down into the executive chair behind his desk. He loosened his tie. His hands began to tremble, ever so slightly.

In the silence of the room the rhythmic ticking of the mantel clock began to draw his attention. He glanced over. The ticking grew louder. He began to perspire and unbuttoned the top button of his shirt.

The sounds of the front lawn sprinklers penetrated the, otherwise, silent room.

Tsk. Tsk. Tsk.

The alternating spray of the railbirds was growing louder, mimicking the repetitive staccato of a rattlesnake.

His hands had grown noticeably trembling. He was on the verge of a full-blown anxiety attack. He tried to concentrate on unanswered letters and long overdue bills but his concentration was shattered.

Fighting an impending panic attack, John Flynn bolted from the room.

CHAPTETR TEN

DECOMPRESSION

She wore only a cowboy hat as she made love to the most famous lawyer in all of Arizona.

In a sleazy, south side motel, Deidre Marie, "Dusty" Carfagno made love to John Flynn. The marine corps tattoo "Semper Fi" was clearly visible on the bicep of his right arm.

She could feel him swell inside her and knew he was nearing climax. She reached over to the nightstand and retrieved the little red pill that waited. Dusty pressed into its side snapping it and releasing its powerful sting.

She put the Amyl Nitrate capsule to her nose and breathed in. Its intoxicant bite slammed into her brain propelling her to her own orgasm. As their passion slaked and he withdrew from her, Dusty lay down beside him, "Oh man, I can always tell … when you lose, it's long and slow and sweet … but Christ, when you win … talk about rode-hard-and-put away-wet."

Flynn's breathing was just beginning to regulate as he tried to justify his serial infidelity.

"After a tough trial, for some guys its drugs … for some it's liquor…"

Dusty knew how easily he grew irritated. She had not intended to annoy him, "I'm not complaining or anything. I think it's kinda cute."

"Cute," he scoffed. "That's a nice word for it."

He paused, thought about what he had just been through. "They hate me for showing them the truth. They were after blood."

"Weren't there other little boys hurt," Dusty prodded. "Five. Raped and murdered…. He do those?"

"I don't know. Nobody does."

"But he could have," she persisted?

Dusty had succeeded in angering him. "Yes … he could have."

"So?" she asked, seemingly confused. Flynn's response no longer hid his annoyance. "That's not what he was on trial for."

Flynn started to get up but Dusty grabbed his hand pulling him back down, "Hey … I'm not sayin' anything."

"Look, I don't know what he did or didn't do. My job was to make them prove what they say he did. I hope like hell he didn't do it, but…"

She pressed to quell his agitation, "Shhh …"

They lay side-by-side quietly. After a minute, Dusty reached over to the little pill box on the nightstand.

"Now, I'm gonna show you some truth," she flirted. For the second time in ten minutes she snapped a red capsule under her nose. She reached to position it under Flynn's nose, but he pushed her hand away.

Dusty kissed Flynn hard on the mouth. He let himself be kissed. She broke off the kiss and began to work her way down his body.

"Oh baby," she whispered, "If you let me … here's what I'll do." Her lips crept down his chest, across his flat stomach. "I'll take care of you."

Flynn felt the liquid glove of her mouth on him and closed his eyes.

Dusty began to moan. "Goddamn it, Flynnie … I love it when you win."

Three days later, they went their separate ways.

* * *

CHAPTER ELEVEN

Not A Lot Of Sympathy For Miranda

The night of Miranda's death had passed slowly for Flynn.

But, at six the following morning, as he did every morning, Flynn dressed and started for the office. Miranda's killing still weighed heavily on his mind.

In a diner near the courthouse he sat chain-smoking, lighting one cigarette with the embers of the prior and stared forlornly into space.

Carroll Cooley sat down opposite him.

The handsome officer plopped a copy of the morning newspaper onto the table. It was opened to the editorial page. There was a cartoon of a man on the gallows. The caption read: "Sorry, Ernie. No more appeals."

Flynn looked up and made eye contact with Cooley.

Cooley shrugged apologetically. "Sorry John. Not a lot of sympathy for him around here."

"He was trying to get his life in order."

Yeah," growled Cooley, "Poor Ernesto. Just a misunderstood sociopath who couldn't catch a break."

Flynn shook his head in compassionate frustration. "He may not have been the most upstanding citizen, but he didn't deserve to die like that. He had a job, and was trying to re-establish contact with his daughter."

"I'll give you this," allowed Cooley. "Never once did he say we had mistreated him in any way. We were doing our jobs. That's just the way it was then."

Flynn didn't respond.

Cooley changed the subject, "Funeral's tomorrow. Saint Anne's."

"They get the guys?" Flynn asked

"Yes. But they made bail and beat it. We think Brownsville."

"Anybody gonna' go get them?"

"Probably not ... like I said ... not a lot of sympathy."

There was an awkward pause in the conversation. Finally, Cooley broke the silence. "Still a lot of interest in us arguing the case."

Flynn shook his head slowly. "No more. Not for me. You get to say it all."

Cooley noticed the metal bracelet on Flynn's left wrist. It had been cobbled together out of prison contraband metal wire. Three numbers;

seven, five, nine, the number of the Miranda case when it was called before the United State Supreme Court.

Cooley tapped it gently, "You've made a difference John. And even though I don't agree with it and probably never will ... you made a difference."

Cooley left.

Flynn sat staring at the bracelet. He began to turn it slowly.

Seven, Five, Nine – "The People of the State of Arizona vs. Ernesto Miranda."

John Flynn lit another cigarette and continued to stare at the bracelet. After a moment, he looked up. The streets of Phoenix appeared the same ... but something had changed.

* * *

CHAPTER TWELVE

THE WOMAN IN THE PARKING LOT

G race Mayberly walked towards her car, arms loaded with groceries. The parking lot was mostly deserted. Only a few late morning stragglers wandered across.

Grace struggled to insert her keys into the car's door lock. She managed to get it open and was starting to deposit her bags inside when without warning something slammed into her propelling her into the car. Disoriented, she turned to see what had caused the collision.

Ernesto Miranda piled into the car and was on top of her. He slapped her hard across the face. "I'm going to fuck you and take your money," he declared.

Grace was shocked and frightened as she struggled to regain her equilibrium. "Look," she said, trying to buy time. "you can have my money ... but if we are going to ... make ... love ... could we at least go to a motel room?"

Miranda was outraged both by the suggestion and her attempt to regain control over the situation. "You fuckin' slut!" he screamed into her face. Miranda struck her a second time. He rifled her purse, stole eight dollars and backed out of the car.

Overwhelmed by shock and humiliation, Grace laid her head back against the seat rest and struggled to regain her composure.

* * *

CHAPTER THIRTEEN

KIDNAP AND RAPE

The words on the movie marque pulsed out into the misty night. It was March 6, 1963.

It was a movie about the Normandy invasion of June 6, 1944 titled *The Longest Day*. It had been based on the novel by Cornelius Ryan.

It was just a little after ten. The theater was empty, allowing Patricia Ann Weir to wrap up and go home a little earlier than usual.

Outside, hidden in the shadows, Ernesto Miranda watched her restack the candy display. He may have been handsome, but in tee shirt and dark glasses he projected the image of a predator.

Patricia was sixteen and blonde possessing an innocent girl-next-door quality.

He had watched her before, but this night would be different. This night the wolf was on the prowl and had prepared for the lamb.

He had arranged two lengths of rope, the ends fashioned into nooses, and attached them onto the front seat of his blue and white Packard. He had draped them over the seat so the noose ends dangled into the back.

His pulse quickened with the excited anticipation of a hunter stalking its prey.

Unaware she was being watched, Patricia set about shutting off the lights, locking the candy counter and setting the lock on the front door. She let herself out and started the lonely walk to the bus stop.

She had not had to wait long. Only a minute elapsed before the city bus swooped her up.

As the bus headed into the night, Miranda's blue and white Packard trailed a few yards behind.

Patricia was tired. She had spent the day in school and the evening at her job. She still had homework for the next day.

Relaxing on the bus, she stared vacantly into space. She was lost in her own imagination and had no sense of what was to come.

She stepped off the bus only a few blocks from her home and stood watching as the tail-light of the bus grew smaller. She lived at the edge of the warehouse district. The houses, while neatly tended, were modest.

At ten-thirty on a weekday night the streets were deserted and eerily quiet. The sense of isolation motivated Patricia to increase the pace of her walking.

She looked around.

The uneven patterns of streetlights and overhanging branches cast ominous shadows along the sidewalk. The absence of sound intruded into her thoughts, the stillness making her wary. Wind blowing through the trees and the sudden rustling of leaves sent chills up her spine, causing her to hurry her pace.

She passed a blue and white Packard parked at the curb, but there was no one in it.

She glanced back over her shoulder. The streets were deserted.

Patricia turned forward.

Miranda was there … out from behind a tree.

She stopped, immediately frozen in fright.

He came towards her. He shook the cuff of his sleeve and a screwdriver slid into his hand. He raised the screwdriver into the soft, pliant, skin of her neck.

It stung.

For a dreamlike moment, they just stared at one another.

Patricia was too scared to run.

When she did not make any attempt to resist, Miranda took her by the arm and pulled her gently back towards his car. He opened the back door and lowered her in. He reached in and placed her hands into the noose-cuffs and pulled them tight.

She was pulled forward until her chest was flat against her knees.

Locked in a prone position, she shut her eyes and waited.

They rode in silence out into the desert.

Twenty miles from town, Miranda maneuvered the Packard down into a gully-like arroyo and turned off the car lights.

In the starless night, darkness was their only witness.

Miranda got out and circled to Patricia's door. He opened it. She did not look up, did not speak, did not protest.

Mistaking her terror for acquiescence, he pulled up her blouse. He pushed up her bra and ran his hands roughly over her chest. She did not utter a sound.

Emboldened, he pushed her onto her side. He raised her skirt and lower her panties. From that vantage point he could see her buttocks, her thighs and her vagina

Miranda had had an erection from the moment he saw her at the movie theater.

He stood for a moment looking at the powerless girl. His sense of power and her lack of protest further fueled his desire. Miranda unzipped his fly and started to penetrate her.

But his elevated state of arousal and the awkward angle at which she lay, caused him to ejaculate before he had completely entered her.

It was over as quickly as it began.

Gently, almost shyly, he redressed her. He untied her wrists and helped her into the front seat.

They drove back to the city, to the spot from which he had abducted her. He pulled to the curb. Leaning across her, he opened the door.

She was free to go.

Patricia started to get out, but he placed his hand on her shoulder halting her progress.

She turned to look at him.

"Pray for me," he said softly and removed his hand from her shoulder.

Patricia got out and closed the door.

* * *

CHAPTER FOURTEEN

OH MY GOD, SHE'S BEEN RAPED

Patricia Walked the last few yards to her home. The lights were out in the modest, sun-bleached, grey, stucco house. The drawn drapes blocked even the slightest sliver of moon light.

Her older sister, Mary, and her brother-in-law Jimmy had gone to sleep.

Patricia let herself in to the darkened house. She went to the kitchen and turned on the light. She was uncertain what to do next.

Patricia went to the sink and turned on the water. She opened a cabinet and removed a glass. She opened the refrigerator but did not take anything out.

The young girl felt disoriented, unable to piece together the necessary components for action. Behind her, the hiss of the running water seemed to grow louder.

The glass slipped from her fingers and crashed to the floor, shattering the stillness of the house.

Mary, came in. She immediately noticed her little sister's clothes were in disarray, "Patti," she asked, "… you okay?

Patricia began to tremble.

"My god, Patti … what's happened?"

Patricia began to weep.

Mary took her hand to comfort her.

Jimmy came in and saw her disheveled condition, "Jesus … what the hell happened to her?"

Patti struggled to speak, "I … I … didn't know him."

Jimmy exploded with outrage, "Jesus-fucking-Christ … she's been raped."

Patti began to sob uncontrollably.

Mary pulled her little sister into a tight embrace.

* * *

CHAPTER FIFTEEN

CELIA

The bell rang at Palmetto Elementary School. First graders by the dozens ran and skipped toward the school. Some held their parent's hand. Others ran on ahead.

One little girl, six-year-old Celia, stood alone.

Far across the schoolyard Ernesto Miranda's blue and white Packard rolled to the curb. He got out.

He saw the little girl and moved down along the fence until it turned to her street. She had her back to him as he closed the distance between them.

She absent-mindedly kicked a soccer ball against the fence, blissfully unaware of her isolation.

Closer and closer he came, until he was almost upon her.

At the last possible moment, she turned.

Her face lit into a big smile and she raised her arms.

"Daddy," she exclaimed.

Miranda knelt on one knee and hugged her. After a brief moment, he got up and took her hand.

Together, they walked into the schoolhouse.

* * *

CHAPTER SIXTEEN

TWILA REBUFFED

Miranda had been awake for almost twenty-four hours by the time he reached home. Twila Hoffman, his common-law wife, was just getting up.

She had been a pretty woman at one time. But life with Miranda had taken its toll. Now, she just appeared tired, worn … worn out.

The house was the untidy mess it always was. Soiled clothing, Celia's half-broken toys and leftover food made up the décor.

He brushed past Twila and entered the kitchen where he removed a mayonnaise jar of a yellowish liquid, home brew he had learned to make during one of his prison stints.

He lifted it to his lips and took a long pull.

Twila moved up to him. It had been a while since they had made love and Twila was feeling the need. Her threadbare bathrobe hung open revealing her nakedness. She leaned up against him and kissed his neck. She pressed her body against his hoping to ignite his arousal.

He tolerated it for a moment, then pushed her away. "I'm tired," he proclaimed. "I'm goin' to bed."

"Where were you all night?"

"Worked a double shift. Goin' to bed," he replied gruffly. He stepped around her and left the kitchen.

Twila had been rebuffed. She stood there feeling foolish, frustrated and humiliated.

* * *

CHAPTER SEVENTEEN

RETURNING TO WORK

Treadaway had been found not guilty on Friday.

The following Tuesday morning, John Flynn strolled into the offices of Lewis and Roca. It was Phoenix, Arizona's largest and most prestigious law firm. They were the epitome of ficus and mahogany. The company logo was etched into the wall above the receptionist's desk.

Giselle, the receptionist, sat beneath the logo in the entrance to the firm.

Flynn's predicable disappearances after a stressful trial were not news to his coworkers. His extra-martial dalliances were a scarcely-kept secret. They were rumored to be the reason for the failures of his previous marriages ... and there had been several.

Giselle, like all the other young females who populated the hallways of Lewis and Roca, found Flynn charming, powerful and sexy. Though they all flirted with him, he had never responded in anything less than the most professional way.

"Good morning, Mister Flynn, welcome back," Giselle cooed upon seeing him. Then added, "We've missed you."

"Thank you, Giselle," he replied, deliberately ignoring her flirtatious demeanor. "Happy to be back."

Outside his fourth-floor office, Wanda Nightingale, the proud bearer of the largest bouffant hairdo in the office, lit up.

"Well, well, well, the wandering prince returns," she said, as he approached.

Used to the little digs from the women in his office, he did not respond.

"Anybody looking for me?" he asked.

"You? No. Only just about half the town."

"Good," he declared with just a tinge of annoyance in his voice. "Then you can tell them I'm back."

He strode toward the office leaving Wanda to shake her head disapprovingly at his back.

He continued into the safety of his office. His secretary, Kathleen, loyal and lovely was how he thought about her, was standing by his desk, sorting through a dozen phone call slips.

"Great. You're back."

"Yes, I'm back. God, can't a guy catch a break?"

Kathleen pursed her lips. "Yes. Poor you. Just the boy who can't say 'no.'"

He was growing annoyed at the constant cadre of disapproving females.

"Anything urgent?" he asked, eager to change the subject.Kat pulled one slip from the bunch.

"This one – Robert Corcoran. Said it was important."

Flynn took it from her, "I'll be back."

"Paul Lewis wanted to see you as soon as you came in."

"Tell him, I'll see him later," he answered, turning on his heels.

Kathleen leaned against his desk and did what all the women of Lewis and Roca seemed to do when dealing with him … she shook her head.

* * *

CHAPER EIGHTEEN

FLYNN TAKES THE BAIT

The polished marble floor of the Maricopa County Courthouse kicked up their reflections as former Assistant District Attorney Robert Corcoran and John J. Flynn strode briskly.

Flynn held a stack of manila envelopes.

It was Corcoran who spoke first. "When I asked the firm to consider two indigent defendant cases a year, I had no idea you were going to turn the whole town on its ear."

"Not to be argumentative or anything," Flynn responded, "but it is just possible that Treadaway didn't do it"

"Yeah," Corcoran conceded half-heartedly, "Possible."

They continued walking, court reporters and law clerks scurried passed them.

Flynn slid one folder from the pile, "Miranda."

Corcoran stopped short, "You're joking."

"No."

Corcoran shook his head in mock frustration. "How about, Hilda Schoenhower," Corcoran asked, with just the faintest whisper of a plea? "Caught her sister with her husband. Shot them both. Temporary insanity – easy."

"Too obvious."

"Oh, now it's got to be 'indigent' and 'subtle.'? How about Henry Smith. 'Mentally retarded,' insisting on being his own lawyer in a second-degree murder case. When does the right of the individual conflict with his own best self-interest and what obligation does the state have in protecting him? Interesting, no?"

"No," Flynn insisted.

Corcoran started walking again, "Come on, Flynn, don't get self-destructive on me."

Flynn grew slightly irritated, "Correct me if I am wrong. Was it not you who had the words: 'Where law ends tyranny begins' etched into the framework above your office door?"

Corcoran shook his head in mock frustration.

"Miranda," Flynn continued to insist stubbornly.

"Oh, that's just great. Their calling it, 'The Mexican who raped the White Girl.' Well, at least it will give the vigilantes of this town something to do. They'll all be circling your house."

Now it was Flynn who stopped short, "That's about the sixth time I've heard that in reference to that case. There's got to be something fundamentally flawed about a case labeled, 'The Mexican who raped the White Girl.'"

"All hell will break loose."

"Yeah. I bet it'll really piss them off," Flynn replied with a half-grin.

Corcoran turned back to face Flynn, "You know, they say, when a person is truly intent on committing suicide, at some point you just have to let go and watch them fall."

Cracking the smile of smug confidence, Flynn walked away. "John Flynn don't fall," he called back arrogantly over his shoulder.

Corcoran watched his colleague depart.

From Corcoran's perspective their hallway meeting could not have gone better. Challenge Flynn, warn him off, and you were sure to ignite his ego and fire up his innate combativeness.

Corcoran strolled along the polished marble floor of the Maricopa County Courthouse. Like the cat that swallowed the canary, he smiled the smile of self-satisfaction.

He had dangled the bait … and Flynn had taken it.

CHAPTER NINETEEN

FIRST MEETING

In the State Penitentiary at Florence, Arizona, the noise never fully abated. It was as much a part of life as flickering light bulbs and facilities that reeked of ammonia.

"Come on, Ernie, you got a visitor," the guard asserted.

He had not been expecting anyone. It had been weeks since Twila had come to see him.

He paced restlessly in the interview room, until a silver-haired man in an expensive suit was ushered in by another guard. John Flynn had come to see Ernesto Miranda.

Miranda eyed him suspiciously. With his tailored suit and abundant self-confidence, he was everything Miranda despised about the establishment.

Flynn extended his hand in greeting, "Mister Miranda, my name is John Flynn. I head the criminal division of Lewis and Roca."

"About fucking time."

"I beg your pardon."

"I been begging for a lawyer ever since they come for me. All I got was, 'Sorry we can't do that.' Now you're here."

Miranda's belligerent attitude raised Flynn's suspicion that he might be intoxicated, not an impossibility in that prison.

"My firm accepts a certain number of pro bono cases a year" Flynn soldiered on, "That means free."

"Yeah?" My last attorney didn't cost me nothin' and I got thirty years."

"That would be, Mister Moore."

"Yeah, Andrew, Adam, somethin'…"

"Alvin."

"Son-of-a-bitch must have been eighty years old."

"Seventy-four, actually."

"Said I should plead guilty by reason of insanity."

"Did Mister Moore actually make any attempt to determine your mental state?"

"What for? I knew I was in Arizona."

"I mean, did he try to assess your mental capacity or frame of mind?"

"All he said was, 'Guilty 'cause of insanity.'"

"Why didn't you take his advice?"

Miranda shifted uncomfortably as he relived his frustrations. "By that time, I had been kicked around all I was going to be. I'd been lied to by the police, told I couldn't get a lawyer and spent six weeks in one jail or another. First time I asked for a lawyer, judge said he couldn't do it. Two weeks later, asked another judge for help – he sez he can't do it 'cause of he ain't got the jurisdiction or some bullshit. Month later they give me what they call a pulmonary something…"

"A preliminary hearing," Flynn corrected.

"Yeah, I tell the judge, look, I don't know how to defend myself. He says he can't give me a lawyer. So, I say, 'Okay, I don't know how to defend myself, so go ahead.'"

"So you waived your right to a preliminary hearing. Then what happened?"

"What do you think happened? In by nine, out by three. Guilty on all counts."

Flynn squinted, feeling he had found a possible avenue of relief. "Well, we feel you may have legitimate grounds for appeal."

"You're too late. I already filed my appeal with the Arizona Supreme Court."

Flynn was surprised to hear that. "You did that on your own?"

"Why not? They got a library and lots of good lawyers in here."

Flynn had heard enough delusional absurdities. He tossed his business card onto the table. "That's my business card. Ask the other 'lawyers' in here who I am. If you need me, call me."

Flynn turned toward the door calling for the guard, leaving Miranda to stare at the business card on the table.

* * *

CHAPTER TWENTY

WESTINGHOUSE

Flynn sauntered into Lewis and Roca. Kat was waiting for him at her desk just outside his door. She held a phone slip between her index and middle finger.

"Paul Lewis. You know … yesterday?"

Without responding Flynn snatched the slip from Kat's finger and turned on his heels.

Emma Sanders, Personal Assistant to Paul Lewis, stood by the fifth-floor elevator waiting for Flynn to arrive. Flynn thought of her as a long cool drink of water. She was beautiful and always perfectly dressed. Emma was the epitome of "professional." For a fisherman like Flynn, she was not only the one that got away, she was the one he would never catch. Emma had boundaries. And in spite of their mutual attraction, it was always just business. For Flynn, it only heightened the attraction.

"There you are. Only one day late," Emma scolded in her gentle way.

"Sorry Emma, personal business."

Emma Sanders had the class not to snicker at what everyone else assumed. She ushered Flynn into Paul's office.

"Mister Flynn, Sir."

Paul Lewis had been reading the newspaper. He looked up as Flynn entered. Lewis was the younger of the two senior partners. He loved the law but loved racquet ball more. When he wasn't in his office, he was on the court.

"There you are. I thought we were getting together yesterday. Missed my five o'clock game."

"I'm so sorry, sir." Flynn apologized. He did not like being scolded.

Paul Lewis dropped the paper to the table.

"Well, you certainly got their attention," he mused with a chuckle.

"I'm sure." Flynn agreed, "The *Arizona Republic* must be having a nervous breakdown."

Lewis nodded, "Oh yeah. Them and a whole lot of other people."

"They mention my name?"

"Did they? I wouldn't read it if I were you," Lewis chuckled again.

"John Flynn, the man they love to hate. It'll be my epitaph."

Lewis changed the subject, "Heard you went to see Miranda. Wasn't he the Mexican who raped the white girl?"

"Seven."

"I'm sorry, what?"

"Nothing, Sir."

"Anything there?"

"He's an interesting case," Flynn allowed. "I swear, I think he was a little drunk. He's angry, belligerent, feels betrayed by the system. I couldn't get a good read on him. I don't think he's stupid, but I also don't think he has the capacity to represent himself in front of the Arizona Supreme Court."

"Is he planning to do that?"

"He's already done it. Filed the appeal anyway. There's nothing there for us."

Paul Lewis digested Flynn's assertion then turned his attention to what he really wanted to discuss.

"Well, I've got some good news. The firm has been retained by Westinghouse Corporation. It's the largest product liability case we've ever handled. Maybe the largest anywhere."

"Great. Congratulations."

"You're going to be a busy guy."

"I look forward to it. But ... uh ... we still owe Corcoran one more 'indigent defendant' case."

"Oh, yes, absolutely ... only maybe ... under the circumstances, we can find something ... a little less awkward."

* * *

CHAPTER TWENTY-ONE

CATCHING UP WITH SCOTTIE

Afternoon traffic and procrastination had gotten him to the public park late.

The baseball game had just ended. Park workers watered the infield and raked the mound. Families headed to their cars.

Only Scottie Flynn, a lone disconsolate straggler, remained. He placed his gear in his bag slowly.

When he looked up, Flynn was standing a few feet away behind the wire screen.

"Hey, Buddy," Flynn called, hoping his son would understand.

Scottie did not reply.

"I know, I'm sorry," Flynn admitted sheepishly, "How'd it go?"

Scottie lifted his head, "I gave up the winning run."

Flynn moved around the fence and sat beside his disappointed son.

"Mom said you would be here," Scottie lamented."

"I had every intention of being here ... only ... I got held up."

Scottie did not react but knew bullshit when he heard it.

Flynn tapped the center of his own chest with two fingers and pointed to Scottie.

Scottie relented, "I know."

Scottie mimicked his father's gesture by point his own finger to his eyes.

"Me too ... only ... once in a while..."

Flynn understood,"I know, I know, Buddy. You're right. But the case is over now and I'll do better. I promise."

They sat silently for a moment. Flynn gazed lovingly at his son. "My father used to say, 'You'll never know how I feel about you until you have children of your own.' And I say the same to you."

"Would Grandpa have liked me?"

"Grandpa would have been crazy about you ... and your brother and your sister."

"I'm not very good at baseball."

Flynn hugged his son, "You'll have better days. Don't ever give up."

Flynn lifted Scottie's bag onto his shoulders. Together they headed towards the car.

If Scottie had been any closer to his dad, they would have been attached at the hip.

* * *

CHAPTER TWENTY-TWO

DINNER DISRUPTED

Camille set the dinner table. She knew John had gone to gather Scottie.

It had been a tough week for her. Camille had been civically active. She had sat on the board of the County Museum overseeing its expansion. She had always enjoyed the camaraderie of the members of their country club. Disturbingly, as the Treadaway case and its resolution hit the newspapers, relationships had begun to change. There had been no more friendly greetings. Finding a golf partner had become difficult. There were glaring glances and whispered conversations when she entered the dining room. And finally, she had returned to her car to find two of her tires slashed.

But he was home now. Her family was intact and things would be alright.

They had assembled for dinner. They all joined hands. John said Grace, "Heavenly Father, we thank you for the blessings we are about to receive."

Scottie added, "Thank you for bringing Daddy back to us."

Camille made fleeting eye contact with her husband.

They all said, "Amen."

"Will you be home every night now, Daddy?" Annie wanted to know.

"I will, Beautiful. Daddy will have regular hours for a while."

"Does that mean you can come to my baseball game on Saturday," Scottie asked hopefully?

"Absolutely. How could you ask such a question?"

Annie interjected, "Well, you missed the last three."

Her accurate accusation irked him.

"Okay, you guys tell me…" He held his hand's palms up, in a weighing motion. "My son, who I love, has a baseball game. Or a man, who I don't even know, will be executed if I don't defend him."

He looked at all three of his children, "Anybody?"

The children sheepishly nodded their understanding. Camille felt irritated by the astonishingly unsatisfactory answer. Even Flynn knew it was an unsatisfying answer.

The usually quiet Michael spoke up, "You really think Treadaway was innocent?"

Camille jumped in, "Michael!" she said in a warning tone that only mothers possess.

"Hey, I've got an idea. When I finish with Westinghouse, we'll go on a vacation."

"Yeah," cheered Scottie. "A real vacation. Not just to Grandma's house."

Flynn reached over and tickled Scottie.

"What do you have against Grandma's house? Wait until I tell Grandma."

Scottie was still very enthusiastic about the idea, "I know. We can go fishing."

Annie scrunched up her nose, "Fishing? Eeeww."

"Let's drive up to the Grand Canyon," Michael offered.

"That's it. We'll go to the Grand Canyon, fishing and eeeww," said John the peacemaker.

Annie giggled.

Scottie pumped his fist into the air, "Yahoo!"

"Or we could stay home and finish the patio project we were all going to do," Camille, the voice of reason chimed in.

Flynn and the kids looked at each other, then reacted in unison.

"Naaahhh."

Camille smiled.

The telephone in the kitchen rang. Camille answered it.

Her demeanor changed instantly.

She extended the phone toward her husband, "It's for you … Ernesto Miranda."

Flynn tried to appear nonchalant as he took the phone from his wife, "Hello."

He listened for a moment, "Tough break."

He glanced towards his family. A chill had descended on the table.

Flynn hung up.

Camille bristled at the breach of family boundaries, "John," she began, as her hand rose to her throat in annoyance and apprehension, "John… How did that man get our home number?"

* * *

CHAPTER TWENTY-THREE

THE LICENSE NUMBER

One week after her abduction and sexual assault, on March 13, 1963, Patricia Ann and her brother-in-law, Jimmy, walked around their neighborhood. With her hands buried in her coat pockets and her head down, Patricia was the picture of disconsolation.

Jimmy, still roiling with rage, was further frustrated by his inability to cheer her up.

They did not speak.

Miranda's blue and white Packard drove by slowly.

Patti lifted her head. Her spirits brightened.

Jimmy noticed. In a voice filled with anger he asserted, "That was him, wasn't it?"

Patti did not respond. She lowered her head again.

Jimmy was furious, "Son-of-a-bitch."

A few minutes later the car rolled by for a second time. This time Jimmy was ready for it. Letting go of Patricia's arm, he darted into the street. Miranda saw him coming and put his foot on the gas pedal. Jimmy got into the street just as Miranda accelerated away. But he saw the license number ... and he would remember it.

On March 13, persistence and effective police work brought Detectives Carroll Cooley and Wilfred Young to 2525 West Mariposa street, where Miranda had recently moved with his girlfriend, Twila Hoffman.

The Packard was in the driveway.

Young peered in the window at the rear seat. He noticed a rope tied around the front and looped over the seat into the back. He nodded knowingly to Cooley. Together, the two Phoenix Police Officers descended on the front door.

Cooley knocked.

* * *

CHAPTER TWENTY-FOUR

A TROUBLED LIFE

Mesa, Arizona, 1947

The morning mist enveloped the graveside shrouding the tombstone in an identifiable haze.

The six-year-old boy fiddled with the buttons on his new shirt. His mother had scrimped and saved to purchase it.

Ernesto Miranda stood beside his father and younger brother as his beloved mother's coffin was placed into the ground. Gravediggers shoveled earth to seal the grave.

Ernesto was frightened.

The one person he loved, the one person really who loved him, was gone. He could only barely grasp the concept of death. The hollow ache in his heart reflected that he understood he would never see her again. She would never hug him or pet his head or murmur his name as he drifted toward sleep. He imagined that if he could just run fast enough, somehow, he could catch up to her.

But how?

Where?

He wanted his father to take his hand, to say something … anything. But the older man stood with his body angled away from his sons. Only the intermittent bobbing of his shoulders gave any indication that their father was crying.

Ernesto Miranda was alone and lonely. He would start first grade at Queen of Peace elementary school in one week. He would wear the shirt his mother had bought for him. He would honor her memory.

He saw no future. Even at age six, anger was the one emotion that would define him.

He had never really gotten on with his father. Manuel Miranda was not an affectionate man. His simple life consisted of work and liquor. Work to feed his family, liquor to numb the ache of unfulfilled ambition. Manuel had migrated to Mesa, Arizona from Sonora, Mexico. He painted houses when he could find any work at all. Raising children, he believed, was work accomplished by women. Consequently, he was close neither with Ernesto nor the younger son, Pedro.

Ernesto passed the next week wandering the desolate streets of Mesa. Kicking rocks in vacant lots or gathering stones to toss at passing cars, he was racked by occasional bouts of uncontrollable sobbing.

School could not come fast enough.

Queen of Peace Elementary school was an exuberant, noisy place. The first day of classes, Miranda was uneasy about mixing with the other children. A young nun, Sister Colondra, noticed him. She thought he was shy but cute. After that first day, she waited for him each morning, smoothed his shirt, made sure his hair was neatly combed and walked him to class. He quickly formed an attachment to her.

Within a year, the elder Miranda would remarry. His new wife, Ernesto's stepmother, would bring neither affection nor solace to the home. The woman drank more than his father. She was an ugly drunk, capable of exploding with sudden fits of rage.

Two years later, Sister Colondra was transferred out of Queen of Peace. The one female who had shown Ernesto affection and compassion had been ripped from his life.

Miranda was devastated … and angry.

It did not take long for him to have his first brush with authority.

To avoid conflict with the school, Miranda developed a high degree of truancy. He would fail to attend school for days, even weeks. He eventually dropped out altogether.

In 1954 Miranda was convicted of his first serious crime, a felony burglary. Two years later and once again convicted he was sent to reform school. Over the next several years he was arrested for assault, burglary, vagrancy, armed robbery and inappropriate sexual touching.

He finally ran afoul of federal law when he was convicted of a Dwyer-Act violation, driving a stolen vehicle across state lines. He served a year in federal prisons in Chillicothe, Ohio and Lompoc, California.

By the time was twenty-one he had a long rap sheet. That was the year he met and began to live with Twila Hoffman. She already had two children.

Together she and Ernesto had another child … a girl.

* * *

CHAPTER TWENTY-FIVE

GROUNDS FOR A FEDERAL APPEAL

Now, they were back in the visitor's room at the Arizona State Penitentiary. Miranda, seething with anger, paced unsteadily.

Flynn was ushered in. He had barely gotten to the table, when Miranda blurted, "The sons-of-bitches turned me down."

"It's all right …

Miranda was not buying it, "Like hell it's all right."

"I mean, that's not the end of the story. I'm here now."

Miranda bristled at Flynn's innate arrogance, "I bet the state of Arizona is just shittin' itself about now."

"We will have to look to the federal courts for remedy."

"How am I supposed to do that? I got no money."

"Nobody's asking you for money."

"You guys are all about the money."

Was it the home brew doing the talking?

"Mister Miranda, have you been drinking?"

"What business is it of yours, how I pass the time here?"

"First of all, it is disrespectful. In addition, it makes it harder for me to do my job."

Miranda struggled to contain his rage.

Flynn returned the file to the manila envelope and got up to leave.

"You called me. I don't ever waste my time."

Flynn was almost to the door when Miranda relented, "Wait."

Flynn moved back and dropped the manila envelope on the table. He was relieved to get a second chance. He knew he had handled the start badly.

"Sit down, Ernie. Let's talk"

It was a difficult internal struggle for Miranda to be even the least bit compliant with authority. But given his limited options, he finally sat.

His next words surprised the agitated attorney. "I been studying the Koran," Miranda suddenly asserted.

The remark caught Flynn off guard. They had not been discussing Miranda's religion. As far as Flynn was concerned Miranda's religious sentiment was irrelevant.

"I thought you were Catholic," Flynn asked anyway.

"I am," Miranda affirmed.

"You thinking of converting?"

"No."

"Then why…"

"I just didn't want you to think I was stupid."

Flynn had been taken off guard, "I…didn't…don't think that."

It was an interesting and revealing look into Miranda's world of insecurity.

Flynn began, "Your file says a lot about you."

"Yeah? Like what?"

"Your mother died when you were quite young. You were frequently beaten by your father. Your father remarried. Tell me about your stepmother."

Miranda's eyes suddenly turned glassy with rage. His glare was so intense that for a moment, it intimidated former combat marine, John Flynn. He had struck a nerve.

Flynn proceeded cautiously, "What was your relationship like?"

Miranda continued to stare angrily at Flynn, "We didn't have no relationship."

"How old were you?"

"I dunno … five … six."

"I mean, when your father remarried."

"Seven … I don't know. I can't remember." His eyes bored through Flynn, as he conjured up the past. It was difficult for him to speak about her. "She would beat us when she got drunk. She got drunk all the time. Didn't matter indoors or out, she got that strap and come at us. I hated it when she hit my brother … and then … there was after…" Miranda couldn't bring himself to go any farther.

"I'm sorry, Ernie. No child should have to live like that."

"Whenever they got money, they drank it. My brother and me never ate on the same day. One day I would eat. The next day him."

Flynn continued to shuffle some papers, "It says in your file you quit school in the eighth grade."

"We never had no money for shoes. When our feet got bigger, we just cut off the ends. I didn't want to get teased all the time, so I just said, 'screw it.'"

"How did you survive?"

Miranda stared at Flynn defiantly.

"By the time I was fourteen, I was thieving full time. You had something I wanted I would cut off your arm to get it."

Flynn absorbed the specifics of the explanation and continued, "You enlisted."

Miranda's tone changed slightly, "I needed three squares and clean clothes. I figured maybe the army would help me sort things out."

"By 'sorting things out' you mean by going AWOL and looking in a woman's window."

Miranda was frustrated to the point he could no longer sit still. He got up and began to pace. The words began to trickle and quickly became a torrent, "The Base Commander's wife used to put on a pretty good show when the 'Old Man' wasn't around. One night we look and she's screwing our captain. He sees me and figures, there's a witness. I got brought up on charges."

Flynn identified the reason he was there, "Ernie, let's get something straight. This case ain't about what a tough life you've had. It's about the law and how it is administered."

Miranda let the words sink in.

"You went to Patricia's neighborhood again, why?" Flynn asked.

Miranda sank to the table and put his head in his hands. He was struggling to articulate the embarrassing truth. "She never fought me in any way. Never even said nothin'. I thought ... I though ... Oh Christ, I thought ... maybe the next time ... it won't be rape."

Flynn just looked at Miranda but didn't respond to the rather remarkable statement.

"I had taken my daughter, Celia, to school," Miranda continued, "I was sleeping. Twila come in.' Ernie, there's police here. They want to talk to you.' They'd seen my car by the house. I went to the door. Twila come up behind me."

Miranda shook his head in frustration, "These two big cops is standing there. Ernie, we want to talk to you and we don't wanna do it in front of your family. I could feel Twila eyeing me. I didn't know what to do. I didn't know whether I had the right to tell those guys to go to hell."

Miranda looked down, sheepishly ..."So I went."

* * *

CHAPTER TWENTY-SIX

THE LINE UP

T he putrid green walls made the room feel oppressive. Patricia's brother-in-law, Jimmy, and her sister, Mary, stood with Patricia Ann Weir behind the two-way glass of the police viewing room.

The four men on the other side were in a police line-up.

Wilfred Young pressed the speaker button attached to the lip of the glass, "Number four. Step forward to the line."

The man stepped forward.

"State your name and place of residence," Young ordered.

The man replied, "Pablo Reyes, Mesa, Arizona."

Young looked to Patricia.

She shook her head and lowered her gaze, "No," she said softly.

Young pressed the intercom button, "You can step back. Next."

Number three stepped to the line.

"Carlos Reynosa, Tortilla Flats."

Patricia shook her head, "No."

"Step back. Next."

Number two stepped forward.

"Alberto Sandoval. Tempe, Arizona."

For the third time Patricia shook her head, "No."

"Number one."

Ernesto Miranda hesitated before stepping forward.

"Number one," Young repeated with a stronger air of authority.

"Ernesto Miranda, Mesa, Arizona."

Patricia stared at Miranda through the glass but said nothing.

Young ached with anticipation, "Patricia," he prodded softly?"

But Patricia just continued to look at Miranda. She seemed almost sad when she turned from the glass, "I don't know … I can't say for sure."

Her brother-in-law erupted, "Jesus Christ, Patricia. That's him. Tell them."

Patricia's sister jumped to her defense, "Shut up, Jimmy."

She held her little sister in her arms as tears welled up in Patricia's eyes, "It's okay, Baby."

Young seethed in frustration.

Jimmy and Mary left. Patricia remained with a police matron.

Young grabbed Miranda from the line up room and led him back to the bullpen area.

Miranda was worried. "How'd I do?" he asked nervously.

Young was frustrated and angry, "You failed," he blurted, "Miserably."

Miranda sagged into the chair alongside Young's desk.

The police matron led Patricia through the bullpen area.

For an instant their eyes met.

Miranda shook his head.

Believing he had already been identified, he foolishly murmured, "Yeah, Man … that's her."

CHAPTER TWENTY-SEVEN

INTERROGATION

Wilfred Young burst into Carroll Cooley's office. "Carroll, you not gonna believe what just happened."

Ten minutes later Young and Cooley hovered over Miranda. They had their jackets off and their guns on their hips. The two giant Redwoods bored in on him.

Young started first. "We know about the lady in the parking lot, the one you slapped around, threatened to rape."

"Why go away for a lousy eight bucks," Cooley overlapped his partner.

"Battery in the commission of a crime will get you thirty years," Young threatened.

"You don't seem like a bad guy, Ernie," It was Cooley playing the good cop, "Maybe we can get you some help."

Miranda perked up, "Help?"

Cooley tapped his finger on his own temple, "You know, help," Cooley suggested.

"You think I'm crazy?"

Young jumped back in, "I think you gotta be crazy to do thirty years for a lousy eight bucks."

Cooley took a more soothing tone, "Why don't you tell us about you and Patricia Ann Weir," Cooley purred? "You've as much as confessed already."

Cooley looked towards his partner, "Maybe if you help us, we can help you. Right Fred? I mean, why file for a lousy eight dollars?" Cooley looked meaningfully at his partner. "Right, Fred? That's a lot of paperwork. What do you think? We wouldn't have to file."

Now, Young-the-closer, raised his voice. "All's I know, if he don't come clean soon, he's gonna get the book thrown at him."

It was Cooley's turn again. "Let us help you, Ernie ... tell us about Patricia."

* * *

60

CHAPTER TWENTY-EIGHT

WESTINGHOUSE

It was late in the day, just around the time Paul Lewis would have liked to sneak away to the racquetball courts. Instead, he sat, legs up on his desk, his face buried in the afternoon newspaper. "They're sending a hundred and ninety thousand American soldiers to Viet Nam," he shook his head in dismay, "That can't be good. Can't be good."

Paul Lewis closed the paper.

He was seated across from a very energized John Flynn. Only moments before Flynn had burst into his office like an enthusiastic puppy. He had been to visit Miranda in prison.

Lewis fidgeted uncomfortably, "John, is there no other worthy case in Corcoran's closet?"

Flynn was excited, "They tricked him into confessing. They lied. He was indigent. Unknowledgeable about his rights."

Lewis was unhappy about revisiting the subject, "I agree, John. Guys probably confess out of fear and confusion all the time."

"Yes. And it's wrong. And, we can help stop it."

Paul Lewis let out an involuntary groan, "What about Westinghouse?" he asked, trying to keep the annoyance out of his voice, "What about Westinghouse? You can't just turn your attention away from them."

"Provide me the resources I need and I can do this and Westinghouse."

Lewis was slowly, reluctantly, resigning to his fate, "You're getting into appellate litigation. You can't alone." He pressed the button on his intercom, "Emma, would you please ask John Frank to join us."

"Yes, Mister Lewis. Right away," came the mellifluous reply.

Just the sound of her voice caused Flynn to lapse into momentary fantasy. He could imagine her sleek, elegant, completely confident manner as she summoned John Frank to join them. He quickly pulled himself back into the moment in order to press his needs, "I will need additional staff."

Lewis was not nearly as confident as the long, cool drink of water on the other side of the door. "This needs to be approached carefully," he said in a voice just bordering on whining, "You'll have the *Arizona Republic* howling at the moon."

As he did so masterfully in the courtroom, Flynn moved in for the kill. "Would that be the same *Arizona Republic* that endorsed our Barry Goldwater. The Goldwater who said 'extremism in the pursuit of liberty is no vice and passivity in the face of tyranny is no virtue?'"

Paul Lewis knew the argument was slipping away from him and grew even more frustrated, "Look, we don't need the *Arizona Republic* railing about a guilty rapist and Westinghouse in the same breath."

Lewis was rescued from the discussion by John Frank's appearance in the doorway. John Frank was a renowned appellate attorney. He wore horn-rimmed glasses and was partial to bow ties. He nodded toward Flynn, "Hello, Flynn. Great work with Treadaway."

"Thanks, John."

Paul Lewis let out an even louder groan, "Can we all agree that we will never utter that name around here again?"

Frank winked at Flynn, "I would think you would relish the notoriety."

Lewis was about to burst with frustration, "Uh huh, uh huh ... right ... relish ... perhaps, you can mention that to Phillip Roca."

Flynn turned to Frank in order to bring him into the conversation, "We're talking about Miranda. They tricked him into incriminating himself. The state has denied his appeal. I believe we'll have a better shot at the federal level."

Frank smiled. "Still obsessed with the underdog, eh? Why stop there?"

"What do you mean," Flynn asked?

"Think bigger. The mountain."

"Supreme Court," Flynn responded?

Flynn thought about it, then nodded, "Now I'm thinking bigger."

Paul Lewis reached for the bottle of indigestion medication that lived on his desk. The discussion had spiraled beyond his control. He needed to stall, to buy time. He needed time to think. He would have to warn Phillip Roca of the boulder that was rolling their way.

"Make an appointment with Rex Lee," Lewis ordered. "He worked for the Supreme Court. He'll have a sense of it."

* * *

CHAPTER TWENTY-NINE

THE TIME MAY BE RIGHT

Within an hour, Flynn had made an appointment with well-known and much respected Phoenix attorney, Rex Lee. His offices were only two floors below Lewis and Roca.

Unlike Lewis and Roca, with its fancy ferns and reflective mahogany, Rex Lee's firm was smaller and less pretentious. It reflected the nature of the man. Lee was handsome, always impeccably dressed and never allowed a single hair out of place.

Lee loved it when other attorneys came in to chat or seek his advice. He was only too happy to meet with John Flynn. They were polar opposites. Lee with his quiet confident demeanor and John Flynn with his larger-than-life personality and unrelenting exuberance.

Flynn had indicated the nature of the visit when he called to see if Rex would meet with him right away.

Lee hurriedly prepared for their meeting by reading about Miranda's original trial. He placed an ash tray on his desk and cracked the window just a little in order to free the smoke that was sure to envelope his office. Therefore, it came as no surprise that when Flynn entered Lee's office, he was holding a lit cigarette between his fingers.

Why not?" Lee began the conversation, "In 1961, when I clerked for Byron White, the Supreme Court heard the case of Dollree Mapp."

Flynn made a lightning speed search of his memory.

"Mapp? ... Possession of pornography?"

"Correct. The police went to her house looking for her boyfriend. They didn't find him but they did find a coffee table book of erotic photographs and arrested her for possession of pornography."

Again, Flynn flashed through his recollections, "Wait, the Supreme Court overturned her conviction. The 'Exclusionary Rule,' wasn't it?"

"Precisely," Lee agreed, "Abuse of power. Cops can't just dislike someone and go on a 'fishing' expedition."

Flynn squinted into his memory, "Fourth amendment?"

Lee nodded, then offered, "The right of the people to be secure in their persons, houses, papers and effects against unreasonable search and seizure shall not be violated."

Flynn brightened, "So, the court said the Bill of Rights applies to the states as well."

Lee nodded again, "And they said it again in 1963 in *Gideon vs. Wainright* – a Florida case."

Flynn struggled to cull his memory, "There was another one. Danny Escobedo. Chicago Police refused to allow him to confer with his attorney in a murder case."

"Yes."

"So, the Court has heard fourth and sixth amendment cases and held that the Bill of Rights applies in state cases."

"Yes," agreed Frank, "But what the Court didn't do is set clear guidelines for police procedure. The police don't have any set of standards to go on. They all just do the best they can."

Flynn nodded his agreement, "That's true."

Lee sought to advise precisely, "So, what I am saying is the time might be right. John, they're a pretty bright bunch up there, but they live an Ivory Tower existence. You've got to shock them. Get their attention."

"Can I do that?" Flynn asked, revealing an uncommon moment of doubt.

"You're the perfect one," Lee reassured him, "But you've got to make them see the blood on the floors and smell the fear in the walls. You can do it. You've been there."

Flynn hurried back up to Lewis and Roca. He found John Frank and together they marched back into Paul Lewis's office.

Lewis was trying to make good on his afternoon escape. He had just shut the snaps on his briefcase when Flynn and Frank breezed back in. He had almost reached the door and their intrusion sent him backpedaling as if he were being held up at gunpoint. He collapsed back into his desk chair and waited.

Like a well-choreographed skit, Flynn and Frank spewed out their plan.

"What's our angle?" Flynn asked, theatrically.

"Fourteenth amendment," Frank supplied.

"Due process. Equal protection under the law," Flynn pronounced.

Frank nodded his agreement, "Yes."

Flynn turned toward Paul Lewis.

"That's it. We're going to petition the Supreme Court. I am going to need at least twenty thousand dollars and all the physical resources the firm can muster."

By that time, Paul Lewis had grown to deeply regret having included John Frank in the conversation. "Great," he acquiesced sarcastically.

Frank grinned a mischievous grin.

"You should probably get word to the *Arizona Republic* before they just hear about it," Paul Lewis advised, looking as if he had swallowed something bitter.

Flynn was energized, "Yes. And I've got to find Corcoran."

Exuding urgency, Flynn hurried from the office.

"Thank you for that," burped Lewis, "If I had just wanted to shoot myself in the foot, I could have done it myself."

The small victory amused Frank, "Come on, Paul. He's excited. Once in a while you've got to reach."

"The timing is not good, what with, Westinghouse and all. Phillip Roca is not going to be happy."

"How many chances does a firm like ours get to petition the Supreme Court?"

Lewis searched for an elusive silver-lining, "Fortunately, ninety-nine out of a hundred petitions for Writ of Certiorari are denied. It'll go away."

Frank turned concerned, "Paul...you're not suggesting..."

Lewis bristled, "I'm not suggesting anything. Just ... get it over with quickly."

* * *

CHAPTER THIRTY

HASSLED BY COPS

The streets were dark as Flynn drove towards the highway that would carry him home.

A police car fell into the lane behind him. After a brief moment, it turned on its flashing lights.

Flynn pulled over.

Two officers, Doran Buhlhesier and Jerry Rivers, approached his car. Rivers hung back and to the side, his hand on his gun.

Buhlhesier reached Flynn's window. He leaned down and ordered, "License and registration, please."

Flynn handed Buhlheiser his credentials, "Something the matter, Officer?"

"We been following you for the last three miles. You been weaving in and out. Please, step from the vehicle."

Flynn got out.

"What is it you do for a living, Mister Flynn," Buhlheiser asked?

"You know damn well who I am and what I do," Flynn shot back – not about to be bullied.

"A word of caution, Mister Flynn. Impeding a police investigation is a felony."

"You giving me legal advice?"

Buhlhesier called over to his partner, "Wasn't there a lawyer named Flynn got that child murderer Treadaway off."

Rivers nodded, "Yup. That was him."

"That's what this is about? You don't approve of the outcome of the trial?"

"That queer killed those other five children."

Flynn was not intimidated in the least, "I think you should arrest me or let me go. Or better yet, you have a problem with what I do for a living, call Carroll Cooley and let him know."

The mention of Carroll Cooley stopped Buhlhesier. He handed Flynn's papers back.

Momentarily mollified, Flynn got back into his car.

Buhlhesier leaned down so they were eye-to-eye, "You be careful out there, Mister Flynn. The streets of Phoenix are a little less safe these days."

* * *

CHAPTER THIRTY-ONE

PARANOIA RISING

Camille was certain she had been followed when she left the country club. She peeked out from behind the curtains on the front door. A dark-colored car drove by slowly. Camille waited. The car made a U-turn and drove back past the house a second time.

She was frightened.

John had always warned her about the rule of three. Even then she could hear his words in her head, "If a car turns behind you once, no problem. If it turns a second time, pay attention. But if it turns a third time, do not pull into the driveway."

Trying to remember if anyone had fallen into that routine, she turned from the window. Headlights splashed across the opposite wall. Nearing panic, Camille looked back out the window. Her husband's car was pulling into the driveway. She sighed heavily and dabbed a lone tear from her eye.

Flynn entered and was startled by Camille who stood right in the doorway, "Camille…"

"Oh, John. Thank god, you're here."

"Why? What's the matter?"

"There was a car…"

"A car?"

"Yes. Driving back and forth … they slowed down."

Flynn took Camille in his arms and kissed on her cheek.

"Okay … shhh … I'll call Carroll Cooley in the morning and tell him. Maybe he can send someone to keep an eye out."

Camille was agitated, "Why were you so late?"

"I was at the office."

"You went to see Miranda again today, didn't you," she asked, sure she already knew the answer.Flynn knew he was about to step on shaky ground. "Yes. The firm is going to represent him in his appeal."

Camille glared at Flynn. It was as if she had been slapped. Fighting her rising temper, she turned and headed for the stairs.

Feeling deflated, Flynn picked up the phone and dialed, "Carroll. You got a couple of guys who love their jobs too much."

* * *

CHAPTER THIRTY-TWO

A QUESTION WORTH
A THOUSAND WORDS

Miranda had been taken from his home and did not return, not that day, nor the weeks that followed. Twila finally tracked him down to the county jail and went to see him.

They sat opposite one another in the visiting room.

"Ernie, what is happening?" she rightfully wanted to know."

"They're holding me on my failure-to-register-for-my-prior bullshit," he declared angrily.

"How long will you be here?"

"How-the-hell should I know?"

"What will we do?"

"You take care of Celia. You be a good mother."

"What will I tell her when she asks where you are?"

He thought for a moment, "Tell her I went to visit my cousin, Felix, in Nogales.

They fell quiet for a moment, and then Twila asked what she really needed to know, "Ernie … What did you do?"

* * *

CHAPTER THIRTY-THREE

MARGUERITE FLORES-REAL

With the energy and exuberance that only a new challenge could create, Flynn went about setting up his new "war room."

Lewis and Roca had provided an empty storage space on the third floor. Tables and chairs were set up. A blackboard was wheeled in. Telephone lines were installed. Flynn oversaw the assembly. Bob Geneson, Paul Ulrich and Roger Kaufman, three exceptional appellate lawyers, completed the five-man team. The table was adorned with foam cups of stale cold coffee and a large ashtray full of smoldering cigarette butts.

John Frank entered with an attractive young Latina.

Her name was Marguerite Flores-Real. Marguerite was a law student of Mexican-American descent. Although she made an impressive appearance, she was uneasy about her current assignment.

"John, say 'hello' to Marguerite Flores-Real. Marguerite is a research intern studying for her law degree."

They shook hands. "What exactly do you research," Flynn inquired?

Marguerite answered as if she had been studying for an exam, "John Flynn, born in Tortilla Flats, star athlete, Combat Marine in the Pacific Theater, University of Arizona Law School, youngest prosecutor in the District Attorney's office."

Flynn nodded, "I get it,"

Marguerite was committed to telling all she knew, "Brought charges against the owners of the *Arizona Republic* for income tax evasion, earned a spot on their 'most-hated' list and a permanent place in their editorial crosshairs."

Frank chuckled.

Flynn shot him an annoyed glance.

But Marguerite was just getting warmed up. "Represented Don Boles, reporter for the *Arizona Republic*, in his divorce proceedings. Was Bole's attorney when he was killed by a car bomb. Tony Adamson confessed to Carroll Cooley of the Phoenix Police Department and was sentenced to twenty years."

"Pretty impressive," Frank beamed like a proud papa.

"Very," reluctantly admitted Flynn.

But Flynn was uncomfortable and eager to change the subject, "So. Marguerite, pretty soon you'll be one of us. You'll be a lawyer."

"Perhaps," she allowed.

"Perhaps. Hmmm. Why just perhaps?" Flynn wanted to know, a bit surprised.

"My view of justice is the guilty belong in jail," Marguerite stated with all the certainty of a forming law student.

Flynn nodded his head, "Can't argue with that. The question for us is, how did they get there? Were they afforded due process?"

Marguerite wasn't completely buying it, "Too many tricks, deals, compromises."

Frank just looked on with a paternal amusement.

Flynn pressed her, "Remember your first year of law school? – Jerky Jernitowski. He fired a gun into a room full of strangers, killing one of them."

She did remember, "Yes. He was convicted of first-degree murder."

"Correct. But why? He didn't know anyone. He had no known motive, not even provable malice. Common sense says, at best, it was involuntary manslaughter."

Marguerite was able to recall, "The court found the act to be so reckless that a reasonable person could have foreseen the outcome."

Flynn was impressed, "Yes. Very good. Exactly. It's not about common sense or street logic. The law views things in its own way. It isn't enough to think a person is guilty, even to know it. You must prove it beyond a reasonable doubt."

Marguerite held her ground, "I have no doubt Miranda is exactly where he belongs."

"That may be true, Marguerite. For us, that's not really the question. Can the average man stand up to the government if he doesn't know his rights?"

Three hours later, Marguerite returned. Arms loaded with files, she placed them on the table in front of Flynn and Frank who had been studying other case files.

"*Carlyle v. Pennsylvania*," she began, "Length of time in custody. *Hamilton v. Massachusetts*. Multiple jurisdictions in a capital murder case. And I could fill the room with denied petitions for legal assistance."

Flynn acknowledged her list, "And there you have the world's most enlightened legal system."

John Frank spoke up, "Sixth amendment. I know it. People must have access to a lawyer, otherwise the government can run roughshod over them."

Flynn was not totally persuaded, "Yes. But they cannot be manipulated into convicting themselves either – fifth amendment."

Marguerite just shook her head, "How does the average person make any sense of all this?"

"They can't. That's why it's the job of the Supreme Court to sort it all out," Flynn assured her.

Marguerite was skeptical, "Funny. In all these files there's no mention of the prolonged emotional state of the victim."

"The law isn't about emotion," Flynn asserted coldly, "It's about impartiality. That's why Lady Justice wears a blindfold."

"Really," asked Marguerite, impertinently, "I thought maybe it was because she was embarrassed."

Flynn took in the comment, "Marguerite, I think your future may lie in being a prosecutor not a defense attorney."

Frank grinned.

Flynn scowled.

Marguerite continued, "I guess I just don't really grasp how a great law firm like Lewis and Roca can invest so much time and this many resources in trying to free a creep like Miranda."

Flynn had the perfect answer, "Because, it really isn't about Miranda the person. It's about the issues his confession represents."

Marguerite tried to absorb Flynn's position. He watched her struggle with his position, so he sought to clarify it, "Look at it like this. A cripple enters the schoolyard; cripple in the sense that he is poor, uneducated and unknowledgeable. There in the schoolyard stands the bully; the bully in the form of the government, all powerful and possessing all the tools of authority, the police, the District Attorney, even the judge. Do we all just stand there and watch the bully pound the cripple? Where is the Noble Soul who will come to his defense?"

"That what you are, Mister Flynn? The Noble Soul?" Marguerite asked with the slightest note of skepticism.

"Marguerite, I don't know if I am noble ... but I tell you this ... I am not afraid of the bully."

Marguerite did not care much for his answer, "How does a raped girl get cast as a bully?" she asked. "The government has to protect her. Your bully is a hero to a lot of people."

Marguerite gathered her belongings and left.

Flynn looked at Frank with consternation, "Couldn't find a research intern who actually likes us?"

Frank cocked one eyebrow and grinned ... "Us?"

* * *

CHAPTER THIRTY-FOUR

AWKWARD DINNER

As they did periodically, the Cooley's and the Flynn's dined in a posh Scottsdale restaurant.

Dinner had been enjoyable though slightly awkward.

Ann Cooley dabbed her napkin to her lips as she finished her dinner. "This place still makes the most incredible Crème Brule."

Camille agreed "John and I have been coming here for years. Never a bad meal."

"Drop of wine left," Cooley advised, "Who wants it?"

There were no takers.

"Now that things have quieted down, maybe you and Carroll can find time for fishing again," Camille said innocently to her husband.

Cooley scowled, "I guess it all depends on your definition of 'quieted down.'"

The words were just sort of thrown out but he was staring at Flynn when he said them.

Flynn picked up on it, "What exactly does that mean?"

Cooley supplied the answer, "The *Arizona Republic* swears you are trying to appeal Ernesto Miranda's case to the Supreme Court."

The mention of Miranda unsettled Camille.

Ann tried to quell the coming disagreement, "Now, boys, let's don't argue."

But Flynn was past listening, "That's right. I am."

Cooley pressed his point, "Don't you think you've done enough to damage the reputation of the Phoenix Police Department?"

Flynn fired back, "Shouldn't you say, haven't you done enough to keep the Phoenix Police from sending a man to death row for a crime that never happened?"

Camille was starting to grow sick to her stomach. "Why don't we go powder our noses," she offered.

The women left the table.

"You know, Miranda was a good bust," Cooley proclaimed, struggling to keep his voice down in the crowded restaurant, "He confessed. Never laid a hand on him."

"No one is saying you did. But…he was tricked. And you did lie to him."

"Are you accusing us?"

"If the shoe fits…"

"We interrogated him. He confessed. What happened to you? You used to be one of us."

"We are simply trying to sort out some constitutional questions. Which might, by the way, help your conviction rate."

Cooley shook his head in frustration, "Look around you. Riots in L.A., women tossing their bras in trash cans, kids burning their draft cards. The world is falling apart, John. Maybe not for you … but for us … its nuts."

"Like the song says, Carroll, 'The times they are a changin'.' After all, Phoenix just elected our first black city councilman. Arizona may make it into the modern world yet."

Cooley looked pained, "But why him? Why Miranda?"

"Why not him?"

"You know anything about him?

"I know what I have read."

The waiter arrived with the check. Flynn reached for it but Cooley stopped him, "No. No. I got this."

Cooley reached down and picked up a manila envelope from the floor alongside his chair. He slammed it down onto the table, "But you take that."

They drove home in silence. Camille was enraged. Her anger radiated across her lovely features and flushed her cheeks.

Flynn needed to address what had happened, "Okay. Spill it."

It opened Camille's flood gates, "You just can't stop. You won't be satisfied until we have no friends."

"Camille, I don't have to pass muster with Carroll Cooley over every case the firm handles."

"We named our daughter after his wife, for Christ's sake. Annie is her god-daughter. It is always you versus something or somebody."

"I am just doing what lawyers do."

"Some lawyers actually pay attention to the needs of their family."

"What are you talking about? Don't I provide for you and the kids?"

"Money? Yes. Time and attention? … do you know that Michael is desperate for your help?"

Flynn was stung, "Michael?"

"He has a crush on this girl at school. He doesn't know how to talk to her. He wants his father's help."

Camille's eyes blazed, "And if there's one thing John, fucking, Flynn knows how to do, it's talk to women."

"Don't start that, Camille."

"Oh? Uncomfortable? How uncomfortable do you suppose it is for me? You think no one knows what a lie our marriage is?"

"That's not true."

"I'm supposed to just stand around and play the little woman."

"I love you and I am crazy about the kids."

"I'm not a victim, I'm an enabler."

"You're a great wife and a terrific mother."

"Don't you dare patronize me with your glib, lawyer, bullshit. It is only, and always, just about you."

Spent silence returned to the car and remained like a hovering raven.

At the house, Camille went straight up to bed.

Struggling against a growing fatigue, Flynn retired to his office. He placed the manila envelope Cooley had given him on the desk.

He sat and stared at it, but ... he could not bring himself to open it.

* * *

CHAPTER THIRTY-FIVE

FLYNN REBUFFS TWILA

Twila came to the door in response to the knock. It was eleven o'clock and she was already working on her third Scotch.

As she did every day until noon, she wore only her threadbare blue bathrobe that she clutched to her chest.

She was surprised to find the handsome, well-dressed man standing in front of her. With his silver hair and rugged good looks, she was instantly attracted. She thought she had even caught a whiff of cologne.

John Flynn extended his hand, "Good morning. May I have a word with you?"

She obligingly stepped back and let him enter.

The place was untidy. The sour smell of unswept dirt clung to the air, but Flynn focused on the reason he had come. He handed her his business card, "Miz Hoffman, my name is John Flynn. My firm is representing Ernesto in his current situation."

Twila gestured for Flynn to sit on the sofa.

She leaned over to retrieve her glass of scotch from the table. Her robe opened revealing her breast almost to the nipple, "Sure. Sit."

Twila leaned over to sweep some clothes off the sofa leaving no doubt she was naked underneath the robe. She poured herself another drink and extended the bottle toward Flynn.

"Thank you, but no. Not the right time."

"Its always the right time for me. Wanna beat a hangover? Keep drinking."

"Yeah. I guess that would work," he agreed, non-committedly.

"You wanna know about Ernie and me," she slurred slightly.

"I'd like to know what happened the night you went to see him."

Twila frowned at the recollection, "He's always tellin' me about Celia."

"His daughter?" Flynn asked.

Twila's eyes flashed, "Our daughter."

Flynn made a mental note of the flash point in their relationship.

"Did he tell you why the police were keeping him?"

"They don't need a reason. Anyway, with Ernesto, it's always something."

For the second time Twila offered the bottle to Flynn.

He waved her off, "No ... really ... thanks."

"It's not easy being alone. "I'm a woman, ya know."

Twila had lost her death grip on the robe. Flynn couldn't help but notice, "Yes ... yes ... you are."

"And a woman has ... needs."

Twila took another sip.

The distraction allowed Flynn time to refocus, "Did he ... uh ... say that he had requested an attorney?"

"He said he asked for lots of attorneys."

"And?"

"And ... everybody said 'no.'" The liquor had taken firm hold of Twila, "But what am I supposed to do? I'm here all alone. I like having a man around."

"Well, maybe he won't be away forever."

She had turned to pick up the bottle. She turned back. The bathrobe was open, all pretense of propriety abandoned. It covered her breasts, but not the beckoning black triangle between her legs.

"I haven't been with someone in a long time, it feels like."

Flynn got up to leave but Twila blocked his path, "You sure you don't want a drink?"

She stepped up to him and pressed her body against his.

Flynn was startled and could feel himself begin to respond but found the strength to push Twila back. Stepping around her, he left the house.

In the car, Flynn loosened his tie. He was perspiring. "I'm not built for that," explaining away his hesitant actions to himself. He gazed at his reflection in the rearview mirror and prided himself on the fact that, for once, he had been the boy who said "no."

* * *

CHAPTER THIRTY-SIX

CALL HOME

With his treacherous meeting with Twila under his belt, Flynn drove back to his office. He had intended to spend the remainder of the day studying the unending pile of legal briefs supplied by Marguerite. There was a handwritten note that had been placed on his chair, "Call home. Important."

Flynn dialed Camille.

As he listened to what she had to say his mood darkened, "Wait ... Camille ... Slow down."

He listened for another brief moment, then, "I'll be right home."

As a man of the law, Flynn was generally respectful of traffic rules. But he broke several of them as he sped to his house.

Annie was in the foyer waiting for him. She was bravely trying too snuffle back her tears.

Flynn knelt in front to of her, "What happened, baby?"

Between hiccuping sobs, Annie told him of her ordeal, "I was walking home. He pulled up next to me. He said I should get into the car. He said ... he said ... 'Your daddy doesn't care about children ... if they get hurt.'"

"Did you get into the car?"

Annie nodded her head as tears rolled down her cheeks, "I had to ... it was a police car..."

Flynn's expression changed, "Did you see the name on his tag?

"It ... it was a long name ... Buuh ... something."

Flynn rose. His look of concern had changed to one of rage.

"John ... John ... no," Camille cautioned urgently.

But she was too late. He was already out the door.

Forcing any notions of right or wrong, good or bad, from his mind, Flynn sped back downtown. He ran two lights, swerved to miss an on-coming school bus and skidded to a stop in front of Sloppy Joe's Café.

Inside, Doran Buhlheiser, Jerry Rivers and Carlton Daynes were nursing drinks at the bar.

John Flynn strode in.

Buhlheiser turned on his stool just as Flynn reached him.

In full stride, Flynn straight-punched Buhlheiser on the point of his chin. He felt the satisfaction of the shock waves rippling up his arm as Buhlheiser went down, taking three other men with him.

Carlton Daynes grabbed Flynn around his shoulders preventing further assault.

Flynn was in full battle mode, "You ever go near one of my children again, I'll rip you to pieces … and you can tell Carroll Cooley I said so."

Buhlhesier tried to respond but his teeth were misaligned. Flynn had broken his jaw. Flynn shrugged off Carlton Daynes and retreated quickly from the bar.

• • •

CHAPTER THIRTY-SEVEN

Outrage in the Rain

I t was night by the time Flynn reached the hallways of Lewis and Roca. He had stopped off at the local hospital. His hand hurt and he had feared he had broken it on Buhlheiser's jaw.

As he hurried toward Lewis and Roca and his temper cooled, he remembered that he had been scheduled for a meeting.

He stepped off the elevator into the near darkness of the hallway.

Paul Lewis startled him. He was standing there with another man.

Flynn's hand had been bandaged before leaving the hospital.

"John. Say hello to Lyle Meyers," Paul Lewis began. "Mister Meyers is chief Counsel for Westinghouse Corporation."

Flynn started to extend his hand then realized the awkwardness. He tried to cover his embarrassment, "Was fixing my car and the hood slammed. Stupid of me."

Meyers and Lewis nodded their understanding, pretending to believe him.

"Painful, I know," replied Lyle Meyers, "Done it myself."

"Mister Meyers stopped by to discuss their case. You remember, we had an appointment," added Paul Lewis, trying to disguise his displeasure.

"Yes. I'm really sorry."

"Quite all right. I just wanted to meet you. Went to law school with your father."

"Oh. You and he were friends?"

"More like friendly competitors. He was a heck of a lawyer, your old man."

"He died the week I graduated law school."

It was Meyer's turn to be embarrassed.

"I'm so sorry. Forgive me for not knowing."

"Quite all right," Flynn forgave him.

"Well, must be running. Nice to meet you, John."

The elevator's return rescued Meyers from the whole awkward encounter. He nodded to Paul Lewis as the doors closed, leaving Flynn and Lewis to themselves.

"Well … nicely done. Why didn't you just spit at him," Lewis asked, clearly irritated.

"He didn't seem that upset," was Flynn's defense.

"That's because he is too much of a gentleman. I assure you Phillip Roca suffers no such affectation. He was here too."

"It won't happen again."

"It had better not. Phillip was extremely upset."

Flynn waited until Paul Lewis had left, then took the elevator back down to the lobby.

A summer squall had kicked up from the desert bringing torrential rain. Flynn stood under the building's front overhang and turned his collar up to shield his neck.

Carroll Cooley stepped out from behind one of the pillars, "My car is at the curb. I'll give you a lift."

At first surprised, Flynn acknowledged his presence., "Am I under arrest?"

"You should be, but you managed to hit the one guy who probably deserves worse."

"A cop puts a scared little kid in a police car for no other reason than to talk about her father?"

"I know. He's suspended without pay. How's Annie?"

"She'll be okay. She's tough. But Carroll, you've got to keep your people away from my children."

"And you stop mentioning my name every time you get mad at somebody."

They nodded at one another in mutual agreement.

"Tell me something," Flynn began, "If you guys really believed Treadaway killed those other children, why didn't you charge him?"

"Not enough evidence."

"So, it is, at the very least, possible, he didn't do it."

"Yes … it is possible. But Miranda is different. He confessed."

"He was tricked."

"You think all we do all day is screw with people?"

"I think every lawyer worth his salt comes into court and claims 'tainted confession' and blinds the jury to all the other acts in the case."

Cooley shifted uncomfortably, "We have the girl's identification in court."

"You give me two hours with Patricia Ann Weir and I will have her identifying *you* in court."

"You look at that file I gave you?"

"Not yet," Flynn prepared to alibi.

"Now might be a good time," Cooley stated.

Flynn hesitated, "Why?"

"The narcotics squad arrested a woman tonight on possession of narcotics with intent to sell. Deidre Marie Carfagno."

"Dusty?"

"Your name was in her address book."

"I represented her in her divorce a few years back."

"That's not exactly the way she tells it."

Flynn connected the words with the subtext of what Cooley was saying, "No, Carroll, No. Blackmail won't work."

"John, listen to me for one second, damn it. It won't take five minutes for somebody in the department to leak this story to the *Arizona Republic*."

Flynn was adamant, "I won't abandon Miranda."

Frustrated and annoyed, Flynn stepped out into the downpour becoming instantly soaked.

"Why haven't you looked at the file?" Cooley called after him, slowing Flynn's retreat.

"Too busy," Flynn called back over his shoulder.

"Bullshit," blurted Cooley, "Too afraid. Once you see what's in it you got no place to hide."

Flynn stopped. His temper flashed, "What is that supposed to mean?"

Cooley reluctantly stepped from the shelter of the overhang, squinting against the rain, "This ain't Treadaway that you can rationalize away by saying the jury set him free. Miranda was guilty. He ain't no poor misunderstood loser. This guy is a full-blown predator. When you do see that file, what's going to be the most obvious is, this ain't about nothing but the enormous ego of John Flynn."

Flynn and Cooley were face-to-face.

"That's right," Flynn bristled, "I want to go to the Supreme Court. And Treadaway was your shot at becoming Captain of the Crime Against Persons Division. So, don't lecture me about ego and opportunity."

The remark stung Cooley but did not dissuade him.

"You know," Cooley retorted, "Somewhere out there in the cosmos, 'the Boy-who-can't-say-no,' and the sexual predator have some things in common."

It was Flynn's turn to feel the sting of truth.

"Yes. You're right. I am not perfect. But I never tried to put someone on death row for a crime that didn't happen."

Cooley grew angrier, his face registering his disapproval. He stepped closer to Flynn to press his point, "Just how desperate are you to see your name in the record books? You can win at the Supreme Court and the cases will get bigger and the women will get prettier, but you will still be chasing the same old demons."

Flynn's eyes bored into Cooley, "My father once told me, never let the big horses trample the little dogs. Right and wrong are not subject to popular opinion. That in my lifetime, I would have to make decisions somebody would not like. 'At no time,' he told me, 'is liberty more precious, than when it is unpopular..'"

Flynn turned and started away. He hunched his shoulders against the downpour.

"Flynn. Wait!" Cooley called, "Get in my car. You'll catch your death of cold."

But Flynn had disappeared into the watery night.

Cooley stood alone, drenched, listening to the sound of the rain splattering against the sidewalk.

* * *

CHAPTER THIRTY-EIGHT

A FULL-BLOWN PREDATOR

Flynn made it to home and warmth a little after ten that night. He allowed himself the luxury of a hot shower. It drove the chill and ache from his body. The bandage on his hand had gotten soaked and he abandoned it.

He donned a bathrobe and retreated to the isolation of his home office. The manila file that Cooley had handed him in the restaurant lay where he had placed it, unopened on the corner of the desk.

Reluctantly, Flynn forced himself to open it.

Its contents revealed that the day on which the information had been compiled, Miranda had been in two fist fights. He had won them both. His rewards had been endless rounds of beer bought by onlookers and sycophants.

By ten o'clock that evening, as he made his way home, he was unsteady on his feet. With his equilibrium went any sense of right and wrong.

He stumbled along a dark residential street. One light spilling from a single window in a house caught his attention. He walked across the lawn and looked into the window.

There was a light on in the bathroom. He could see a woman, naked in front of the mirror, toweling her hair. She was not memorably pretty. His only attraction were her visible breasts.

Fueled by the abundance of beer and completely divorced from reality, Miranda moved unsteadily to the front porch. He walked up the steps and tried turning the doorknob. It gave. It was unlocked.

Emboldened by the booze, he brazenly proceeded in. He crossed to the foot of the woman's bed. The woman was just coming out of the bathroom.

When she saw him, she gasped and froze in fright.

Miranda stepped forward and took her by her hair. He led her to the bed where he forced her down on to all fours.

The woman began to whimper, "Please. Please. Let me get under the covers."

Ignoring her pleas, Miranda placed himself behind her and continued his assault.

His body aching and his mind reeling, Flynn closed the folder. He lowered his head to the desk and placed his hands over his head.

Cooley had been right.

Miranda was a full-blown predator.

* * *

CHAPTER THIRTY-NINE

"You Been Goin' Out"

Twila had not been to visit Miranda in months. She finally went to visit him.

She was nervous and uncomfortable in the jail surroundings.

She was also concerned about Ernie's disposition under the circumstances. She did not have to wait long to find out.

He was angry. "Took you long enough to come see me," he began before she had even settled in her chair.

She tried to alibi herself. "Ernie, I been busy with Celia."

But he would not buy it. He shook his head vehemently. "You been goin' out."

Twila tried to defend herself. "What do you mean, 'goin' out'?"

"Running around. Seeing other guys," Miranda accused

"That's not true."

"You think I don't know. Even up here, I hear things."

"No. No," she protested, "It's not true."

"You don't act like a good mother. When I get out of here, I'm gonna come for Celia."

Twila was gripped by anxiety. "I'll never let you take Celia."

Miranda's rage ignited. He jumped up. "When I get out … I'm comin' for Celia."

Twila was frightened into cringing silence. Even up there, surrounded by glass and guards, she was frightened of him.

* * *

CHAPTER FORTY

THE FINAL STRAW

The next morning, Kathleen was waiting for Flynn by the elevator. Before he could step off, she handed him the slip of paper summoning him to Phillip Roca's office.

Phillip Roca was the firm's elder statesman and majority partner. White hair and skin tanned by days on the golf course, he was a large, imposing presence in any room. He was generally soft-spoken, but that day would be a definite exception.

Flynn caught up with Paul Lewis as he reached the fifth floor. Together they soldiered towards Phillip Roca's office and his wrath.

Phillip slammed the morning newspaper onto his desk, "It isn't enough you embarrass the firm, and skip meetings jeopardizing our relationship with Westinghouse, now you have to be associated with this sleazy prostitute or call girl or whatever she is." He railed at Flynn, "We've provided means and manpower and this is what we get?"

"You firing me, sir?" Flynn wanted to know.

His answer only added fuel to Phillip's fire.

"Don't be insolent with me, Flynn," Phillip barked, florid-faced, "You're lucky the only thing I hate worse than bad publicity is the way the *Arizona Republic* does politics."

Flynn held his ground. Without flinching he said, "It is a personal matter, sir, that should have no bearing on our relationship with Westinghouse."

Phillip fired back, "That's where you're wrong. It has everything to do with Westinghouse.

Flynn felt trapped and a little desperate, "This is a once-in-a-lifetime chance to go to the Supreme Court."

But Phillip Roca was not having it, "The Supreme Court may feed your ego, but Westinghouse feeds our families. Drop it," he ordered in uncertain terms.

"So, you are firing me."

Phillip nodded, "We will no longer finance or support the appeal. If you wish to pursue Miranda, you will do so at your own expense, in your own offices, away from Lewis and Roca and with whom-so-ever wishes to work with you."

Paul Lewis placed his hand on Flynn's arm, "Think about it, John, before you answer."

But Flynn was Flynn, "I don't have to think about it. You knew who I was when you asked me to join the firm. I am not a guy who ducks every time someone fires a shot across my bow."

Phillip Roca closed the conversation, "Fine. Then have your letter of voluntary withdrawal on my desk in the morning."

With nothing else to say and no more room for argument, Lewis and Flynn retreated from Phillip Roca's office.

Once in the hallway, Paul Lewis tried to balance the realities of their position and his empathy for his favorite attorney, John Flynn, "I'm sorry, John. The article was the last straw."

Flynn nodded his understanding, "Me too. I never meant to bring any harm to the firm."

Lewis tried one last lonely time, "In all Corcoran's closet of horrors, is there no case of some old lady who poisoned her husband?"

Flynn smiled his appreciation, "In all Corcoran's closet of horrors, there is no other case that strikes at the heart of our constitution the way Miranda does."

* * *

CHAPTER FORTY-ONE

ALONE

Flynn arranged for and opened his own office away from the firm. His fellow attorneys struggled to work between the two offices.

For Flynn, with his own money at stake, the offices were much smaller, the desks far fewer. Gone was the coffee maker, the printer and all the other accouterments of the firm's backing.

Frank and Flynn struggled to find the perfect presentation for their petition to the Supreme Court. They concentrated on establishing the reason the court should grant the writ.

Frank wrote a line, decided it wasn't quite right, squashed it into a ball and tossed it disdainfully across the room. Crumpled balls of yellow lined paper and abandoned coffee cups littered the room.

They lost track of time.

They listed ten cases relevant to their position, but it was their closing conclusions with which they hoped to attract the court.

"There is little about the petitioner or the crime for which he stands charged that commends itself. But the cause of due process is ill-served when a disturbed, little-educated indigent is sentenced to lengthy prison terms largely on the basis of a confession which he gave without being first advised of his right to counsel. This petition, therefore, squarely raises the question of whether the right to counsel turns upon request; whether, in other words, the knowledgeable suspect will be given a constitutional preference over those members of society most in need of assistance.

We respectfully ask that certiorari be granted and the judgment of the court below be reversed. In view of the fact the Escobedo decision has been misapplied, we would further ask the court to reverse the judgment summarily."

Believing they had, at last, made the best possible appeal, John Frank signed the petition. He handed the pen to his colleague and friend, John Flynn.

Brimming with hope, Flynn took the pen and signed his name on the second line.

* * *

CHAPTER FORTY-TWO

WRIT OF CERTIORARI

Flynn had gone out to purchase another carton of cigarettes.

His new office had only one window that he never opened. The result was the office was overcome with a brownish-yellow haze. John Frank wrinkled his nose when he entered. The residue smoke irritated his eyes and he waved his hands as if trying to clear a space where a person could breath.

Flynn was not there and Frank was not about to stand in the mist and the acrid annoyance it caused. He stepped back into the hallway and bumped into the returning Flynn.

"There you are," said Frank. Then added, "How do you live in there?"

"What do you mean," asked the totally oblivious Flynn.

"That can't be good for you."

Flynn did not respond to Frank's stern judgment, so Frank moved on to the reason for his visit.

He handed Flynn an envelope, "You should read this."

Flynn tossed it disdainfully to the table, "I will … later."

Frank persisted, "You ought to read it now."

Frustrated by Frank's intrusion, Flynn picked it back off the table.

It bore the logo of the United States Supreme Court. Flynn ripped it open and perused its contents.

One line jumped out: "In the matter of the people of the State of Arizona versus Ernesto Miranda, writ of certiorari is … HEREBY GRANTED."

It took Flynn a second to process what he had just read. He read it a second time. He looked up at Frank. Frank was smiling.

"Hollee…" uttered Flynn, "Hollee…"

"Congratulations."

"Oh my god," Flynn said again.

Frank tried to restore a moment of reality, "There will be companion cases. Stewart, Vignera and Westover, Attorneys General from all four states, New York, Ohio and all."

"Yes. Yes," Flynn agreed.

Frank continued, "The ACLU will want to file an amicus brief."

"I know," Flynn agreed, "All time-in-custody and right-to-counsel cases."

"True," sympathized Frank, "But you'll be first on the docket. You've done it. You're going to the mountain."

Flynn blinked as he thought about what Frank had just said, "Wait a minute… We've done it. We're all going."

Frank began to look uncomfortable. He looked down for a moment before he spoke, "I'm afraid, I won't be."

Flynn couldn't completely grasp what Frank was telling him.

"The firm has made it clear that any prolonged absence on my part renders less sure the notion that my place will be available."

A rolling sensation in his stomach made Flynn feel as if he has been punched in the gut, "I see."

Frank looked as if he was in physical pain, "I'm sorry John."

Flynn understood, "You don't have to apologize."

"I'm too old to start over."

"It's okay, John. I understand. I really do. It's just … it won't be the same without you."

"But you can do it," Frank encouraged, "You'll be great. Only stick with sixth amendment. Lawyer. Lawyer. Lawyer. It's what they'll want to hear."

Marguerite had come in during their exchange making the same smoke-clearing arm wave as Frank. Her arms were loaded with additional case files. She dumped them on the floor. "I maybe be able to bring you some stuff after work," she said, joining their conversation.

Frank put his fingers to his ears, "I don't think I should be hearing that."

Flynn and Frank hugged briefly. It was an awkward and embarrassing moment. Marguerite looked away as if to allow them privacy.

Frank left.

Marguerite seemed to struggle to gather her words, "I know I haven't been very supportive, but I'm sorry it's come to this."

Flynn nodded his agreement and understanding, "Mark Twain once said, 'Reports of my demise have been greatly exaggerated.'"

Marguerite smiled at his doggedness.

Flynn suddenly succumbed to an uncharacteristic moment of self-doubt, "But what if I'm wrong?"

"Wrong about what?"

"All of it. Treadaway. Miranda. The way the police operate."

"How can it be wrong," Marguerite asked, "if it's only about fairness?"

Flynn squinted as he absorbed her words of support. It had only been a brief moment of insecurity. "You're right, I suppose. At least, we've gotten their attention. This is our chance to shed some light on the uneven process of justice."

"Right," offered Marguerite cheerily, "Sixth amendment it is."

"Yes. But ... um ... you know, Marguerite, John's probably right. But, maybe you can find a fifth amendment case or two ... just in case."

Marguerite agreed, gathered her belongings and started back out. She passed Lyle Meyers just coming in.

"Mister Meyers," Flynn greeted in surprise.

"Was on my way to see Phillip when I heard the news. I just stopped by to say congratulations."

"Thank you. You are a majority of one."

"Why do you say?"

"I seem to have alienated just about everyone."

Meyers seemed sympathetic, "The road to justice can be bumpy."

Flynn dropped his emotional guard, "Lyle, you said you knew my father."

"Yes."

"What would he have done?"

Meyers pondered the question before speaking, "Jack was a terrific lawyer. But he was pragmatic and very savvy. He would not have done what you've done."

The air seemed to go out of Flynn. He bowed his head towards the floor, "I see."

Meyers lifted him with his voice, "But John, I really stopped by to tell you how pleased we are to have been represented, however briefly, by the man who would take the Miranda case to the United States Supreme Court."

Flynn thought for a moment. The big guys understood. "But the firm has distanced itself from me."

"Yes," confirmed Lyle Meyers, "It was our request."

Flynn thought about it for a second, "I see."

They shook hands and Meyers started to leave, "I have to admit, Jack would have been very proud of you."

Flynn was alone. He needed to mentally regroup. He took solace from Meyers' words of admiration. He picked up the letter and read it again. He closed his eyes and breathed deeply.

"I am going to the mountain," he said aloud, "The mountain. The mountain."

Across town in the parking lot of their golf club, Camille waited for the tow truck that would rescue her car. She had gone to lunch at the club, dined alone and was working on her third martini when someone slid the afternoon edition of the *Arizona Republic* across her line of vision.

She had paid the check and beat a hasty retreat toward her car. All four tires had been slashed. Camille waited for the tow truck, her emotions careening between anger and fear. The overwhelmed wife was gripped by a deep sense of resentment towards her husband.

* * *

CHAPTER FORTY-THREE

NEAR DEATH

Flynn's continued work separated him from his family. His lack of presence enveloped the family like an unwanted shroud. Night after night, they ate alone.

Flynn worked in his office, slept in his office.

The sense of abandonment grated on Camille. Her patience with the children had grown shorter as her bouts with alcohol grew longer. She was constantly on edge.

Her social isolation, at the club, also struck deep into her sense of well-being.

She felt increasingly vulnerable. In her mind, every passing car brought with it the potential of some aggression towards her or her family. She had become dependent on sleeping pills to make it through the night.

One night, as she lay in bed waiting for the pills to take effect, she thought she heard a sound emanating from downstairs. Fighting the fog of chemically-induced slumber, she got up and moved to the top of the stairs. She strained to hear if it was more than her imagination.

There was definitely a sound.

Someone was in the house.

Alarmed to the verge of panic, Camille tip-toed down to the foyer and slipped into John's office. In the drawer of his desk she found his pistol.

Camille hated guns. She feared them and the awesome destructive potential they possessed. But this was her home. Her children were upstairs asleep in their beds. Her maternal instincts outweighed her trepidation.

She checked the bullet chamber to be certain it was loaded, then slipped it into her bathrobe pocket.

She tip-toed across the foyer toward the kitchen.

The sound had grown louder. The kitchen light was lit. The refrigerator door was open, blocking her view of the intruder.

She raised the gun, aimed it at the space just above the door and cocked the trigger.

Michael, her eldest son, poked his head up from the protection of the refrigerator door. He saw his mother and the weapon pointed at him.

"Mom ... Jesus. Mom. It's me, Michael."

The gun dropped to her side, "Oh, my God, Michael. I ... Oh, my god."

Camille fell back against the kitchen wall. Tears escaped beneath her tightened lids.

She had come within a hair's breadth of shooting her own son.

* * *

CHAPTER FORTY-FOUR

LAST PLEA

Although it seemed forever, the time had come. Flynn was as prepared as he would ever be. His bag was packed. He waited for the cab that would carry him to the airport. He fought a strange combination of excitement and dread. He knew he was ready but was cautious about the unexpected.

As he waited, he reviewed his carefully honed opening presentation for the hundredth time. He could hear John Frank's words of advice in his head: "Lawyer, lawyer, lawyer. Sixth amendment." But a piece of him felt the unmistakable tug of the argument against self-incrimination and that meant fifth amendment.

He heard footsteps and assumed it was his ride coming to collect him. He was surprised when Camille walked in.

"Camille," he said in a voice that clearly rang with confusion, "You didn't have to come out. I am going to take a cab to the airport."

She answered in sober voice, "I didn't come to drive you to the airport."

He looked momentarily confused.

"I came to ask you not to go," she said.

He looked at her. "How can I do that now," he asked trying to hide his rising frustration.

"Because its what's best for your family."

"Please, don't do that Camille. You know I care deeply for my family. You know that."

Camille struggled to maintain her composure, "I don't even know Miranda, but I feel violated by him."

"Camille, I'm a lawyer. I'm doing what lawyers do."

"I'm afraid to be alone."

"I'll be back in three days."

Camille shook her head as if to shake off his previous remark, "I don't mean that kind of alone. I ask myself … is it me?"

"Is it you, what?"

Her voice trembled, "I know you have been with other women. But I took a vow … made a commitment."

It was the worst of all conversations to have at that moment.

"Look, Camille. I know I have a lot to answer for. I know that. When the case is over, we'll take the kids. Go away."

She teared up, "I never really will be Mrs. John Flynn, will I?"

He embraced her, "Please, Camille. Don't do this now. I need to stay focused. Hang in there just a little longer."

Camille backed out of his embrace. She started to turn back out of the office, "I'll tell the kids you love them."

Alone again, Flynn battled the conflicting emotions of guilt, anger and insecurity. He needed to regroup. Camille had upset him. He needed to focus. It was too late to turn back now.

After a minute, with resolve returning, he picked up his suitcase to go.

Marguerite was in the doorway, "I think I just passed Mrs. Flynn," she observed.

Marguerite was holding an envelope, "I came to wish you luck ... and to give you this."

She handed Flynn the envelope.

"What is it?" he inquired.

"I thought, while I was at it, I'd do some background work on Earl Warren."

Flynn chuckled at her audacious tenacity, "And?"

"You may want to sit down."

Flynn looked at his watch. He did not have much time. He leaned his haunches against the end of the table.

Marguerite began, "Before he was the Governor of California, he was the District Attorney of Kern County."

Flynn nodded, "Yes, I knew that."

"His own father was murdered. Detectives from his office went out and found the guy who did it and beat a confession out of him."

Flynn's lower lip curled up, "Didn't know that?"

"Warren refused to use the confession in prosecution because of the way it was obtained. In other words, it was coerced. The killer went free."

Flynn processed the nugget Marguerite had provided.

He smiled, "Marguerite ... you're a genius."

* * *

CHAPTER FORTY-FIVE

THE MOUNTAIN

Washington, D.C., February 28, 1966

The overnight flight to Washington was long and bumpy. Unable to sleep, Flynn played all the elements of his presentation over and over again in his mind. He was headed for the grandest stage and his greatest moment. It was hardly the sort of event that allowed one to just close their eyes and doze.

A smattering of snow blanketed the sidewalk and covered the steps of the United States Supreme Court.

Inside, F. Lee Bailey argued the case of Doctor Sam Sheppard.

Flynn watched from the wings.

The gallery was packed. Rockefellers, Kennedys, even numerous congress persons.

As Bailey passed him in the hallway, Flynn drew a deep breath.

Flynn, the Master of Summation, was born to hold center stage. And this … was his moment.

The Marshal guided the appellants into the court.

The robed justices walked in and were seated.

A chant rose up within the court:

"The Honorable, the Chief Justice and the Associate Justices of the Supreme Court of the United States. Oyez! Oyez! Oyez! All persons having business before the Honorable, the Supreme Court of the United States, are admonished to draw near and give their attention, for the Court is now sitting. God save the United States and this Honorable Court."

Butterflies winged through Flynn's stomach. They swooped and swirled and flapped in frenzied flight.

Flynn glanced at the appellee's table. Frank had been right. It was packed. Attorneys General and ACLU lawyers crowded together. John Frank sat in a row nearby.

It was his moment Flynn and he was ready.

Chief Justice Earl Warren called the appellants before the bench. "Number Seven, Five, Nine, Ernesto A. Miranda, petitioner, versus Arizona."

Flynn approached the podium. There were three lights attached. Green to begin, yellow to summarize and red, the absolute stop-point.

The green light went on.

Flynn drew a deep breath and began. "Chief Justice, may it please the court. This case concerns itself with the conviction of a defendant of the crimes of rape and kidnapping and robbery and kidnapping."

As Rex Lee had predicted, the justices sat up just a little straighter.

"The facts in this case indicate that the defendant was a twenty-three-year-old of Spanish-American extraction who, on the morning of March third, 1963, was arrested at his home and taken down to the police station by two officers named Cooley and Young, and interrogated. He denied his guilt at first according to the officers but by 1:30 PM confessed. I believe the record shows that at no time during the interrogation, was he advised either of his right to remain silent, his right to counsel, or his right to consult with counsel."

Justice Abe Fortas was the first to jump in.

"I am sorry to interrupt, Mister Flynn … but did you say he was not told that he might remain silent?

"Yes sir. That is correct,"

"Please, continue."

Flynn did not miss a beat.

"My position is simply this, that the State of Arizona has imprisoned this courts' Escobedo decision by refusing to apply its principals in this case. I would like to observe that this court in the Escobedo case set forth the circumstances under which a statement would be admissible."

Carroll Cooley and Wilfred Young stood outside Miranda's front door.
Miranda stepped out.
"Ernie, we have some things we'd like to talk to you about. We'd like you to come with us."
Miranda was uncertain.

Twila stood behind him in the doorway.
"Standing there, in the doorway, I didn't know whether I had
the right to tell those guys to go-to-hell."

Fortas was staring at him. Flynn continued, "One, the general inquiry into an unsolved crime must have begun to focus on a particular suspect."

Miranda waited in a line-up. He was number one amidst four.

"Two: A suspect must have been taken into custody."

A badly frustrated Wilfred Young led Miranda from the line-up
theater to an interrogation room.
"How'd I do," Miranda asked.
Angry, Young replied, "You failed, miserably."
Miranda slouched in his chair.
A Police Matron led Patricia Ann Weir towards another inter-
rogation room. Miranda glanced at Patricia. For an instant, they
made eye contact. His expression turned to sorrow.

"Three," Flynn explained, "The police in their investigation must have elicited an incriminating statement."

"Yeah, Man," Miranda murmured sadly, "That's her."

Flynn was in rhythm. Standing straight at the podium he continued, "Four: The suspect must have requested and been denied an opportunity to consult with his lawyer. And five: The police must not have effectively warned the suspect of his constitutional right to remain silent. When all five of these factors have occurred, then the Escobedo case is a controlling factor."

Justice Potter Steward leaned toward his microphone.

"How would you define adversary proceeding?" Stewart asked.

Flynn replied, "At the point where he is the focus of the investigation and the questions asked are for the purpose of his conviction. A man who is poorly educated is, at the very least, at that stage of the proceeding to be represented by counsel."

Stewart came right back at Flynn, "What would a lawyer advise him his rights then were?"

Flynn had anticipated the question, "That he had the right not to in-criminate himself. That he had the right to be free of further questioning by the police. That he had the right, at the ultimate time, to be adequately represented by counsel and that if he was too poor to employ counsel, the state would furnish him counsel."

Stewart was approaching the question most fraught with peril, "What is it that confers the right to a lawyer's advice then and not at an earlier point. Would it be the sixth amendment?"

Flynn could hear John Frank's voice in his head. The argument that never ceased: "Sixth amendment, John. Lawyer, Lawyer, Lawyer."

Flynn was at the water's edge. He was about to cross the Rubicon. If he chose wrong, all their efforts, all the tears and toil, could be imperiled. But Marguerite had provided him an enormous insight.

He drew a deep breath, "No ... the attempt to erode or take away from him the fifth amendment right already existed, and that was the right not to convict himself."

Stewart pressed him further, "Would he not have had that right earlier?"

Miranda stood in his doorway opposite Cooley and Young. Twila stepped up behind him.

"Standing there in the doorway. I didn't know whether I had the right to tell those guys to go-to-hell ... so I went."

Flynn answered Stewart, "Yes ... If he knew about it. And if he was intelligent and strong enough to stand up against the police interrogation and request it."

"Was there any claim that his confession was compelled or involuntarily taken?

"None at all, your Honor. In the sense that anyone forced him to do it."

"Well, was it voluntary or involuntary," Stewart pressed.

"Voluntary, in the sense that he was not mistreated or threatened. Involuntary in that he never knew he didn't have to tell them anything."

"You would say his fifth amendment rights were violated?"

"I would say his fifth amendment rights were violated."

Justice Byron White weighed in, "Because he was compelled to do it?"

"In the sense Your Honor is using the word "compelled. Your Honor is correct."

"I was talking about the constitution and if he was compelled to do it. "

Justice Hugo Black interjected, "That doesn't mean he has to have a gun pointed at his head."

Justice White argued back, "Of course, he doesn't. But still, he was compelled to do it. Is that not right, Mister Flynn, according to your complaint?"

Flynn nodded, "Not at gunpoint, as Mister Justice Black has indicated. He was called upon to surrender a right he didn't really appreciate that he had."

Justice Black pressed on, "Control and custody. Why would that not tend to show some kind of coercion? Was he allowed to get away after that, at will?"

"No, your Honor. He was confined under arrest."

At that point, Chief Justice Earl Warren entered the conversation, "I suppose you would say, Mister Flynn, if the police had said to this young man: 'Now, you are a nice young man and we don't want to hurt you and so on and so on. We are your friends…'"

Cooley and Young hovered over Miranda. Guns on their hips clearly visible, they bored in, "We don't want to see you go away for twenty years for a lousy eight bucks. "You help us, we'll help you."

Warren continued, "…and if you will only tell us how you committed this crime, we will let you go home and we won't prosecute you. That would be a violation of the fifth amendment and would not, technically speaking, be compelling him to do it."

Flynn's spirits began to brighten. Warren got it!

"It would be an inducement," Warren continued, "Would it not?"

Flynn was certain he had gotten through, "Yes, Your Honor. That is right. And a form of subtle coercion."

Warren nodded, "I suppose you would argue that it is still within the fifth amendment?

Flynn sensed connection.

"It is an abdication of the fifth amendment right."

"That is what I mean," said Warren.

Warren looked around, "Well, Mister Flynn, it seems we have used you to express our various perspectives on the issue. It seems only fair, under the circumstances, that if you should desire additional time, it be granted."

For an instant, Flynn was a deer caught in the headlights. More time was the last thing he wanted. "Uhh … well … umm … thank you, Your Honor. But, I don't think that will be necessary."

A smattering of compassionate laughter rippled through the gallery.

The yellow light on the podium came on.

"I would like to state in conclusion that the State of Arizona has, in its constitution, provided for its citizens, language precisely the same as the fourth amendment to the federal constitution as it pertains to searches and seizures."

As was his way, Flynn paused, setting up for the conclusion, "I simply say that unless the court takes a firm position it will be another fifty years before the full scope of the fifth amendment, will reach the state of Arizona."

The red light came on.

"Thank you."

Flynn walked back to the Appellee's table and sat down. He looked around as if only first noticing the assembled gallery of spectators.

Smiling, he took a deep breath and was washed by the emotional sensation of fulfillment. He had done it ... been to the mountain.

* * *

CHAPTER FORTY-SIX

HOMEWARD

The Warren court heard the cases of Miranda, Vignera, Stewart and Westover for two days. By sundown of the second day, the fine dusting of snow that greeted John Flynn upon his arrival at the court had dissipated. What little snow remained had been swept to the sides.

A man stood at the bottom of the steps as the excited attorney descended. As Flynn approached, the man held out his hand.

"Mister Flynn. A fine job in there."

"Thank you, Sir," Flynn responded appreciatively.

"F. Lee Bailey," the man said by way of introduction.

"Yes. I recognize you. Pleased to meet you," said Flynn, "You did a pretty good job in there yourself."

"Not my first time here. Still, it's a pretty intense experience."

"Indeed. They know their stuff."

Bailey chuckled, "Time to unwind. Let it go. How you getting home?"

Flynn thought for a second, "Gonna fly back to Phoenix soon as I can."

"If you want, you can hitch a ride with me. I'm flying back to Los Angeles tonight."

For an instant Flynn didn't really grasp the invitation.

"On my private jet," Bailey added. allowing Flynn to fully understand the offer.

Flynn smiled, "Sure ... why not?"

The Lockheed Jet Star, billed itself as the Cadillac of private business jets. The high-end jet cleared the clouds and settled into its cruising altitude of twenty-five thousand feet. The party was in full swing. A few well-dressed gentlemen and several exceptionally pretty women clustered around the bar, champagne glasses in hand. The activities had started the moment the aircraft left the gate.

John Flynn had become the center of attention. He relived the excitement and exhilaration of appearing before the justices of the Supreme Court.

He drank, he spoke ... but, mostly ... he flirted.

Cooley's prediction had already begun to come true. The cases would get bigger ... and the women were already getting prettier.

* * *

CHAPTER FORTY-SEVEN

SHE'S GONE ... TAKEN THE KIDS

True to his word, Flynn returned to Phoenix three days later. Still flushed with pride and brimming with satisfaction, he opened the front door to his home fully expecting the usual rush of joyful children. This time would be special. This absence meant he would be returning as a player on the world stage.

Camille's car was not in the driveway.

Flynn put his key in the lock and let himself in.

"Hello. I'm back. I'm back," he called from the foyer.

His enthusiastic exuberance was not returned. The house was strangely quiet.

There were no gleeful children rushing to greet him.

He entered the kitchen. Gone were the pictures on the refrigerator, Scottie in his baseball gear, Annie in her soccer uniform.

With a sinking feeling in the pit of his stomach, Flynn rushed to the children's room. The walls were bare, no pennants, no perfume, no personal effects.

Camille was gone ... had taken the kids.

Flynn sank down on Michael's bed. The air went out of his exuberant balloon as if he had been hit in the gut.

His triumphant return had been dashed by the reality of their departure.

* * *

CHAPTER FORTY-EIGHT

MIRANDA OVERTURNED

Florence, Arizona

June 13, 1966 was just another day at The Arizona State Penitentiary. The constant wall of incoherent voices wrapped like a blanket around men in captivity trying to endure yet one more day in confinement.

Up on the third tier, Ernesto Miranda leaned his head against the bars listening to the cacophony of noise. Through the chaos one sound caught his attention.

It sounded as if people were calling his name: "Ernie. Ernie. Ernie,"

But maybe he was only imagining it. He strained against the bars hoping for a clearer identification.

There it was again.

Then one booming voice cut through the chaotic clutter

"Ernie … You just be overturned."

What had the voice said?

"Ernie … You just been overturned."

There it was again; louder, clearer, unmistakable. Other inmates caught the message. Their voices grew more unified. "Ernie, Ernie, Ernie … you just been overturned."

Miranda closed his eyes and banged his head against the bars as the chants washed over him.

"Ernie. Ernie. Ernie."

* * *

CHAPTER FORTY-NINE

ALONE

Flynn lay on the one remaining piece of furniture in his house.

Empty wine bottles surrounded the couch.

His inattention to his personal grooming had resulted in a three-day stubble.

The phone rang. He reached down and answered it.

It was John Frank, "Congratulations, John. You've won."

But Flynn remained subdued. He barely lifted his head off the arm rest. "How about that?"

Frank was excited, "You've just improved America."

"Have I?" Flynn asked, enduring the pain of a cruel irony.

"Thanks, John … See ya."

Flynn let the phone slip from his fingers back down to the phone's cradle. He draped his arms across his face and closed his eyes.

What should have been his moment of greatest triumph, felt like a bad joke with an even worse punch line.

He had improved America … And unraveled his own life.

The phone rang for a second time.

It was Miranda. He was still in prison. Flynn listened to his client's lengthy lament. Flynn sat up straight. With each angry syllable Flynn's expression tightened. Finally, having vented as much venom as he could, Miranda slammed down the phone.

Flynn stared straight ahead absorbing Miranda's words of righteous indignation.

Now it was John Flynn's turn to dial the phone. He glared into space, as the buzzing on the line seemed to go on forever.

Finally, "John Frank here."

"Oh my God, John. We've goofed. I mean we have really goofed."

"Oh?" asked a surprised and skeptical Appellate Attorney.

"In our enchantment over the rape case we completely overlooked the assault in the parking lot. He's still in jail."

"How is that?"

"We never argued the parking lot case."

"Oh my," Frank replied.

John Frank thought before speaking, "Well fortunately the old traditional rule is that if a confession is truly involuntary, you know, I mean, the rubber hose or pipe, it was excluded under old traditional grounds."

"Yes," acknowledged the agonizing Flynn, "But the State of Arizona will feel they've been burned by Miranda."

"Then you will have to file a writ of habeas corpus in the federal court. And John, you had better find a sympathetic federal judge."

"I'll have to get a federal judge to agree that his second confession was involuntary under traditional standards."

"Yes. That will force the state to grant a second trial on the woman in the parking lot case."

"Okay. Yes. You're right."

Flynn hung up. He lowered his face into his hands, "Oh my God. I can see the front page of the *Arizona Republic*: 'Miranda' can't help Miranda."

* * *

CHAPTER FIFTY

MIRANDA RELEASED

Miranda sat in the first row of the Coach Car. He was finally on his way home.

He was neatly attired in a suit and tie. His hair had been trimmed by the prison barber. The newspaper with his picture and the words, "Miranda released" rested on his lap.

He was returning to a hero's reception … he was certain of it. There would adoring admirers, cheering crowds and hangers-on eager to ply him with drink.

The train pulled into Tempe station. Miranda disembarked.

A rolling tumbleweed, blown across the parking lot by an early spring breeze, was his only companion.

The station was deserted, a scheduling mistake, he was sure.

In reality, no one cared about Miranda the man. It was only by chance that the decision bore his name.

Miranda was forced to confront the reality that his delusional moment of fame and glory was not to be.

* * *

CHAPTER FIFTY-ONE

FLYNN AND MIRANDA MEET

Three weeks after Miranda's return to Phoenix, he and Flynn met on a warm Sunday morning on the rooftop of the Wayward Ho. It was the tallest building in Phoenix.

Miranda spoke first. "Thought I might never get out."

"We got lucky. We found the right federal judge."

"You guys fucked up," Miranda accused.

"Yes," Flynn reluctantly agreed. "We made a mistake,"

"So, you guys ain't perfect."

"No," Flynn was forced to admit in a rare moment of modesty, "…not perfect."

Miranda had put on weight. He now wore black–rimmed glasses.

He stood with his face tilted towards the sky while John Flynn leaned on the railing a few feet away.

"The sun feels good. Warm." Said Miranda. "I was always cold inside."

"What will you do now?" Flynn wanted to know.

Miranda thought about his answer. "I want to find Celia. Get her back and live out my life in peace."

"You'll need a job. Proof of paternity."

"I can do it. I will do it."

"I believe you will."

"I learned some drafting inside. Maybe I could get a job. Meanwhile, I haul produce at a warehouse," he said shrugging.

They lapsed into momentary silence. Then Miranda spoke, "What about you?"

"I've started my own firm," Flynn replied. "Something will turn up."

Miranda looked at Flynn with an uncustomary moment of affection. "We had something you an' me, right?" Miranda asked with the slightest hint of pride. "They'll always remember my name."

"Yes." Acknowledged Flynn. "For once, you got lucky, I suppose. If the companion cases had not been Stewart, Vignera and Westover, the Miranda decision might bear someone else's name. I mean, after all, M is the thirteenth letter of the alphabet."

Miranda accepted the explanation of just how much serendipity had played in his questionable notoriety. He quickly changed the subject from that uncomfortable reality.

"Your family?" he asked Flynn.

"What do you mean?" Flynn questioned.

Miranda shrugged off the question's significance. "I hear things." was Miranda's non-committal explanation.

"I'm going to catch up with my kids. Help Annie with her math."

Miranda thought for a moment.

"We had something, you and me, huh?"

"We did at that."

"They will always know my name."

Flynn nodded in homage to the truth of his statement. "They will always know your name."

"An' that's something, right?"

Flynn nodded again, bowing to the truth. "Oh, you bet."

Miranda reached into his coat pocket and withdrew a silver bracelet. It had been made out of prison contraband. Pieces of wire had been fashioned into the numbers: Seven, Five, Nine. He handed the bracelet to Flynn, "I had time while I was waiting for the court to decide."

Flynn was touched by the gesture. He accepted the bracelet and secured it around his wrist.

"They will always know your name," said John Flynn.

* * *

CHAPTER FIFTY-TWO

DEATH OF A FOOTBALL STAR

Several months passed.

Arizona State had just crushed its in-state rival in a football game. In the shadow of the football stadium, at a local athlete's hangout called the End Zone, people celebrated. It was Saturday night. A party was in full spring. Coeds danced, drank and flirted. The jocks reveled in the spoils of victory.

The star quarterback, the very handsome Tommy Johnston, sat at the bar, enjoying the fruits of a five-touchdown game. Numerous admirers plied him with shots of Tequila. By ten o'clock, he was feeling no pain.

It was an unlikely setting for what was about to transpire.

The Fragile Sparrow, Daniel Treadaway, slithered into the bar and onto the vacant stool alongside Tommy Johnston. "Hey. Hi … you're Tommy Johnston, right," asked Treadaway like a star-struck groupy?

"Fuckin' A," was Johnston's inebriated response.

"Quarterback, right? You had an amazing game today," Treadaway flirted.

"Yeah," Johnston grunted in agreement. "Pretty fuckin' amazing."

"I'd like to buy you a drink." Treadaway offered. "Can I buy you a drink?"

"Sure. That's what I'm here for."

Treadaway blushed and smiled his best smile.

* * *

CHAPTER FIFTY-THREE

DEAD ON THE COUCH

Three hours later the night air was cut by the shrill urgency of police sirens. Flashing red lights strobed through the night air. Police cars were positioned diagonally toward the curb in front of the athlete's dorm.

An ambulance stood nearby.

Uniformed officers questioned potential witnesses. They had seen Tommy Johnston go into his apartment with another man. He was slender, much smaller than Johnston, was all they could remember.

Inside his apartment, the scene was horrific, so bloody even seasoned detectives were forced to look away. Tommy Johnston lay splayed across the couch clad only his underwear, his torso half on the couch, half on the floor. Blood everywhere. The back of his head had been bashed in, having been struck repeatedly with a blunt object.

Tommy Johnston was dead.

The police got the description they needed. Daniel Treadaway fit the bill. They fanned out and searched for him. He was discovered as he left another downtown bar. He was quickly gathered up and run in to the police station for further interrogation.

Doran Buhlheiser hovered over the badly frightened Daniel Treadaway, "I'm not going to say it again, you little faggot. We know you killed Tommy Johnston. Now say it."

Treadaway was uncommunicative and badly frightened, "I ... I ... don't know what happened. I ... I can't remember."

Buhlheiser punched Treadaway on the side of his head knocking him to the floor. Treadaway lay there momentarily, dizzy and disoriented.

Buhlheiser reached into his desk draw and withdrew a length of thick rubber hose, "See this?' I'm gonna break every bone in your body. Never leave a mark."

Treadaway tried to slide back away from Buhlheiser. The cop continued to stalk him until Treadaway was cornered.

Buhlheiser struck Treadaway with tremendous force.

Treadaway screamed.

Buhlheiser leaned close to his cornered suspect and yelled into his face, "Say it. I killed Tommy Johnston."

Treadaway lay on the floor too terrified to respond. Buhlheiser struck him on his leg again. Treadaway screamed again.

"Say it, god damn you." Buhlheiser yelled.

Buhlheiser lifted his arm to strike one more time. Treadaway raised his arms in hope of shielding himself from the blow.

"I ... I ... want to see my lawyer. I want to see my lawyer!" Treadaway screamed.

Caught in mid-fury, Buhlheiser hesitated. He was in unchartered waters.

"I want to see my lawyer!" Screamed Treadaway again, his voice quivering.

* * *

CHAPTER FIFTY-FOUR

TREADAWAY AND FLYNN ... AGAIN

There was the sound of ringing.

In the dark, he could not be sure it was real. It seemed very far away. But, as it persisted, it seemed to draw nearer.

Finally, Flynn reached out and picked up the phone, "Huh…yeah?"

He listened as the party on the other end articulated their reason for calling. The words pulled him upright on the couch, "Pick me up."

Ten minutes later, Marguerite pulled to the curb in front of Flynn's house.

Flynn was dressed in slacks and a sports jacket by then. He got into the front seat. Marguerite made a U-turn and they headed for downtown Phoenix.

"Thanks for doing this," Flynn appreciated.

"I just answered the phone."

"What were you doing in the office at this ungodly hour."

Marguerite smiled shyly, "What I always do when I can't sleep."

Flynn allowed a small smile for his fellow compulsive personality, "What have they got?"

Marguerite spelled it out as best she could, "They were seen together at The End Zone. That's a bar near campus. Tommy Johnston was the quarterback. They were seen entering the kid, Johnston's, apartment building around midnight."

Flynn was incredulous, "Treadaway killed a football player?"

"They've got him downtown. Did you meet Tommy Johnston in the End Zone bar? Yes. Did you go back to his apartment? 'Yes.' Did you and he argue? 'Yes.' Did you kill Tommy Johnston? 'I want to see my lawyer.'"

Marguerite chuckled, "Boy … you really *must* piss them off."

Flynn was severely aggravated, "Piss them off? I risked my reputation for Treadaway. I lost my family with Miranda. I alienated all my friends, my family, my colleagues."

Flynn lapsed into seething silence.

They arrived at the downtown police department.

"Don't wait," Flynn instructed. "I'll get a cab home."

Fueled by aggravation, Flynn marched purposely into the harsh fluorescents of the Phoenix Police Department. He by-passed the front desk, opting instead to head straight to the interrogation room, a trip he had taken hundreds of times.

Carroll Cooley waited outside. He raised his hands to slow Flynn's progress, "Before you go in there, I need to let you know he got a little scuffed up during the arrest."

Flynn nodded his sardonic understanding, "Slipped while trying to escape?"

"He resisted arrest."

"So, in addition to killing a football player, Treadaway took on the Phoenix Police Department? He must be a whole lot tougher than I ever gave him credit for."

"He was about to confess."

Cooley made the sign for "one inch" by holding up his thumb and forefinger, "We were this close. And Flynn ... he's not getting off a second time."

Flynn stepped around Cooley and into the interrogation room.

As Doran Buhlheiser had promised, Treadaway did not look as bad as he felt.

"Daniel," Flynn said by way of greeting.

Treadaway could barely make eye contact, "Hello, Mister Flynn."

"Didn't realize you were still in town. Thought you had gone to your mother in Kingman."

Treadaway was slow to answer, "I probably should have."

Fighting a swirling tide of anger, Flynn strained to move the interview along, "Care to tell me what happened?"

Treadaway seemed to be organizing his thoughts, "I was in this bar. This guy started talking to me. He said he had some sports stuff he wanted to sell, if I was interested."

"You met a guy at a bar and you went back to his apartment?"

Treadaway looked away to avoid Flynn's stare, "Yes."

Flynn was struggling against a rising rage.

"We were drinking ... a lot."

"And you made a pass at him, which he rejected."

Treadaway, looked down, embarrassed. He nodded the slightest, "Yes."

"That's okay, Danny. We're past all that ... I'm going to ask you something I have never asked a client in my entire career," Flynn hesitated, "Did you kill Tommy Johnston?"

116

Treadaway looked up with puppy-dog eyes, "I don't know."

The answer ignited the rage that had been boiling through Flynn's veins, "You don't know?" he bellowed. "You don't know? I got drunk, don't know what I did with the car keys. Spent a night with a chick, can't remember her name. But 'I can't remember whether or not I killed some-body'? You son-of-a-bitch."

Treadaway was frightened by the intensity of Flynn's outburst, "I ... was very high and very drunk. I passed out. Outside of Maginty's. I remember looking up at a bunch of cops. They were yelling at me and throwing me around. And there was ... a lot of yelling."

Flynn's fists were clenched as he leaned toward Treadaway, "And you said ... 'I know, I'll call that nice man that got me free last time.' And, 'I'll just say ... I can't remember.' That how it went? ... Huh?"

Treadaway was growing frantic, "They brought me here. They kept hit-ting me and yelling at me. I seen in the papers what you did for that guy, Miranda. I said, I wanted to talk to you."

Flynn kicked the chair he had been sitting on. It went skittering across the room, "You wanted to talk to me?" Flynn bellowed, "Well, here I am. Talk to me. Did you kill Tommy Johnston?"

Carroll Cooley stepped into the room, "Counselor..."

Cooley's intrusion was enough to break the adrenalin of anger con-suming Flynn. He looked down at his clenched fists.

He had come one length of rubber hose away from becoming Doran Buhlheiser.

Flynn stepped back and unclenched his hands.

Treadaway continued, almost pleading to be believed, "They stopped hitting me. But they were still yelling when they went outside. I was scared of them."

Flynn collapsed into another chair opposite Treadaway. He lowered his head into his hands, "What a joke. My first client, is the last guy I ever thought I would see."

Treadaway raised his hands to his face and wept behind his fingers.

* * *

CHAPTER FIFTY-FIVE

MIRANDA SEARCHES FOR CELIA

For days and nights, Miranda wandered the streets of Tempe searching for Twila and Celia. He looked in every bar and down every alley. He scoured school yards and church rectories.

Then, one day, out of sheer blind luck, he walked into a supermarket and there they were.

Celia spotted him first and sought refuge behind Twila's skirt. Twila looked up, saw him, panicked and began to yell, "No. No. You go. Go away!"

Miranda's relentless search had culminated in that moment and he would not be dissuaded. "I told you I would come for her," he stated darkly.

"No," Twila yelled as loud as she could.

Her anguish caught the attention of a young stock clerk who foolishly tried to intercede.

The clerk raised his hand in front of Miranda to ward him off.

Thirty years of street violence had taught Miranda that the surest resolution to any conflict was the first swing. Miranda punched the clerk, sending him sprawling into a display rack of cereal boxes.

The brief altercation provided Twila and Celia just enough time to flee.

The Manager dialed the police.

Miranda ran out.

* * *

CHAPTER FIFTY-SIX

FAMOUS

Miranda continued to search for his common-law wife and their daughter – convinced he had come one step closer to his goal. One unusually cold day as Miranda wandered the streets, a police car pulled onto the sidewalk blocking his path. The officer got out and confronted him.

Miranda waited warily for the officer to speak.

"You are under arrest for the kidnapping and rape of Patricia Ann Weir."

Without any time to process the command or come up with an alibi Miranda turned around and allowed himself to be cuffed. He was, by then, familiar with the drill.

The second officer began to read from a small index card; "You have the right to remain silent. Anything you say, can and will be used against you in a court of law. You have the right to be represented by counsel during questioning. If you cannot afford an attorney, one will be provided for you."

They started to place Miranda into the squad car.

Miranda hesitated and looked back at the officer, "Can I ask you a favor?"
The officer seemed impatient with the delay. "What's that?"

Miranda looked at him hopefully, "Would you read that again?"

The officer seemed annoyed. But the second cop thought for a second. He seemed to have made the nexus, "Hey, Charlie … I think this here … is the guy.

"What guy?" the first officer wanted to know impatiently.

"You know…the guy."

The first officer thought about it for a moment and finally made the nexus, "Oh … Uh" the Officer began awkwardly.

"Could we…uh…would you sign this?"

* * *

CHAPTER FIFTY- SEVEN

FLYNN AND MIRANDA – SECOND TIME AROUND

Two days after Miranda's re-arrest Buhlheiser, Rivers and Carlton Daynes lounged in the back room of Sloppy Joe's Café. They were detoxing from a long night shift.

Daynes had the morning papers spread out on the table, "Look at that. That bastard Flynn is gonna represent Miranda again."

"That son-of-a-bitch used to be one of us," Buhlheiser spat.

"This has got to end," Jerry Rivers lamented. His boyish face had started to show signs of age and stress.

Buhlheiser shook his head, "He won't be happy until he's dragged the entire department down, made us look like fools to the public."

Daynes held his lips together tightly, "Not enough he handcuffed us. Now he wants to thumb his nose at everybody."

"He has got to be stopped," Buhlhesier asserted.

"This has got to end."

•••

CHAPTER FIFTY-EIGHT

SETUP

Flynn was naked and flat on his back. Dusty's cowboy hat covered his face as she straddled him. Beads of perspiration rolled slowly between her perfectly shaped breasts.

Holding a rolled-up dollar bill to her nose, she leaned over and snorted a line of cocaine off a small hand mirror on the night-stand, "Sure you won't join me?"

"Positive," Flynn confirmed, "You're going to kill yourself with that crap."

"Oh … but what a beautiful sunset it will be."

Flynn shrugged her hat off his face and struggled to a half sitting position leaning on his elbows. He was frustrated, "I can't do this anymore."

Dusty looked hurt.

"It's not you, Dusty," he reassured her, "I need to get my life in order. A 'new leaf' sort of thing."

She leaned down and kissed him on the lips, "I'm not a school-girl anymore, Flynnie. I knew you could never love a girl like me. Besides, I'm likely to be away for a while. I don't suppose you'd like to tell me how you'll wait for me."

"Get yourself a good lawyer."

"Any suggestions?"

"My old firm used to have lots of them."

Dusty eased herself off him.

Reluctantly, he let her go.

They sat on the side of the bed next to one another. Flynn stared at the floor forlornly, "She left. Took the kids."

"Can't blame her. What did you expect?"

"I was a lousy father and a worse husband."

"Sometimes children can forgive. "

"Too bad we can't see into the future."

"I've seen it," She declared, sardonically, "It's overrated."

She opened her little red pill case. She offered a small capsule to him.

"Come on, Dusty," He declined, moving his head away.

"It'll make our last time memorable."

"Every time with you was memorable."

"Oh yeah, the silver-tongued devil," she purred.

She snapped the capsule and placed it beneath her nostril. Her head jolted back. She tried one more time to locate the capsule under his nose, but the overwhelming odor of ammonia repelled him.

He pushed her hand away. "Dusty," he said with finality, "it's over."

Her car was parked around the corner in an alley. Dusty left the building and walked to her car. She got in and looked into the rear-view mirror. Carlton Daynes lay draped across her back seat. The shadows from the alley partially cloaked his face.

"He didn't go for it," Dusty informed him.

"We took a shot. It didn't work, that's all."

Dusty thought for a moment. She sighed sadly, "I'm gonna miss him."

Daynes did not answer.

His silence worried her, "We still got a deal … right?"

CHAPTER FIFTY-NINE

License Challenged

One month later, Flynn sat, looking like a scolded school-boy, on an ancient wooden bench outside the Arizona Bar Association Licensing Board.

Charges of drug use and prostitution had been levied. His license to practice law had been challenged. People walked out and passed him but still he waited. Only when the stream had become a trickle did Robert Corcoran emerge.

Stomach roiling with apprehension, Flynn stood up.

Corcoran approached quickly.

"Well?" Flynn asked, unable to contain his anxiety.

"Insufficient evidence," Corcoran blurted, "You get to keep your license."

Flynn let out an audible sigh of relief. He hugged Corcoran.

Corcoran continued, "They took a shot and missed. But believe me, John. It wasn't because they didn't try."

Flynn nodded his agreement, "I know. I know. Thank you, Robert."

Flynn turned to go.

Corcoran interrupted his retreat, "Want a piece of advice, John?"

Flynn turned around, "What's that?" asked the newly emboldened attorney.

"For once ... just once ... stay out of the schoolyard."

* * *

CHAPTER SIXTY

REJECTED

Paul Lewis was waiting for Flynn when he got off the elevator. "Heard the good news. Congratulations."

"Thank you. It was nerve wracking."

"I'll bet."

They walked together to Phillip Roca's office.

"You dodged a big one," was Phillip Roca's term of greeting.

Flynn was purposeful, "You said, when the time was right, I could rejoin."

Phillip seemed to ponder the remark for a moment, "Yes. When the time was right."

"But now is the time. We've won at the Supreme Court. Momentum is on our side."

"On our side?" Roca repeated, incredulously, "We've been left with the remnants of angry clients and a vengeful, politically-biased, newspaper conglomerate."

Roca's lack of agreement angered Flynn, "Get me off the ship and raise the gang plank. That all that was?"

"We had to fill your position and with the number of clients we lost, we are not in a position to hire for its own sake."

Flynn was incredulous, "For its own sake? Like I'm a stranger?"

Paul Lewis, eternal peacemaker, sought to modulate the tone of the conversation, "John, you may have won more than you know. The decision has jarred loose a cognition that the entire legal system is in need of an overhaul. They've started to form a blue-ribbon committee made up of judges, legal scholars, prosecutors and attorneys. They named this fellow Warren Burger to head it."

Phillip Roca's tone softened considerably, "We have placed your name in nomination to the committee."

"What does that have to do with me?" Flynn asked.

Lewis smiled, "Your rightful place in history," was his reply.

Lewis and Flynn descended to the cafeteria. Seated at a table in the eatery, Flynn could barely touch his food. "Now, when I need them the most … I'm just out."

Lewis seemed resigned to the reality, "What did you really expect? You have upset the applecart pretty good around here. The police are furious. The *Arizona Republic* is furious – and the state feels it's had its laundry aired on the national stage."

"They're wasting their time. His original confession is inadmissible."

Lewis begged to differ, "They've got Twila."

"Twila?"

Lewis laid it out for Flynn, "She'll say: 'I went to see him after he was arrested.' The prosecutor will ask, 'And what did he say?' My guess is, what she says he said will sound remarkably like his original confession."

Flynn argued back, "So, they'll coach her. She's a known welfare cheat."

Lewis was much more pragmatic, "But she's who they will have to believe if they want to convict him. It's not just 'the Mexican who Raped the White Girl' anymore … Its 'Miranda' now."

Reluctantly, Flynn had to succumb to the harsh truth, "So, the State of Arizona will have its pound of flesh."

Lewis tried to be encouraging, "You've done all you can. You have achieved a monumental victory. The laws of this land will be administered more fairly because of you. Get on with your life."

"And let him go into the schoolyard all alone?" Flynn sighed the sigh of resigned truth, "That's not who I am."

* * *

CHAPTER SIXTY-ONE

CONFRONTATION

Flynn trudged on alone, working late into the night. He was the Saint of Summation. He needed the perfect close for Miranda's retrial. He worked until his mental ergs ground to a halt. His body ached from fatigue. Finally, he organized his writings and secured them in the desk draw.

He locked the office door and rode the elevator to the lobby. The building was deserted. He stepped out of the building and started for his car, the only one in the lot at that hour. He could instantly sense something was wrong. Some sounds of silence brought soothing, others apprehension. It was an instinct honed in the bloody battles of the Pacific, the sense that your enemy was close by.

Almost to his car, Flynn turned … and there they were.

Doran Buhlheiser, Jerry Rivers and Carlton Daynes were coming towards him. And all three carried wooden ax handles.

There was nowhere to run and no desire to succumb.

He placed his back to his car, effectively cutting off one avenue of attack.

He was John J. Flynn, ex-Combat Marine. And anybody who thought his Marine Corps tattoo was just some New Year's Eve drunken water-color, had badly misjudged.

Buhlheiser swung first.

Flynn caught the blow on his forearm, stepped forward and punched. His assailant went down.

The others swarmed in. One to the ribs and one to the shoulder and Flynn was propelled back against his car. Buhlheiser punched Flynn on the side of the head. Rivers slammed his ax handle across Flynn's chest.

Daynes charged Flynn, striking him in his midsection and knocked him back against his car.

Flynn droves his knee into Daynes chin.

Flynn punched Rivers. Rivers landed hard.

Buhlheiser swung his ax handle

Flynn ducked, but was clipped on the forehead. He stepped into his punch to Buhlheiser and Buhlheiser went down.

Blood flowed from the Flynn's head wound. His lip was cut and there was a rapidly growing mouse under his right eye.

Struggling to his feet, Flynn used the door handle of his car to right himself for the next assault.

He came back at them, hitting Rivers on the side of the head. He swung at Daynes and missed, allowing a counter-punch to his gut. He took it and kept on swinging.

Buhlheiser had gotten to his feet. He came forward and caught Flynn flush on his cheek. Flynn shrugged it off and surged forward. He caught Rivers coming in and Daynes just before he started to back away.

Blood spurted.

But the fight suddenly stopped.

They were in a standoff. Huffing and struggling for breath, Flynn sought to take the psychological advantage. "That ain't bad for round one."

Rivers cast a furtive glance toward Buhlhesier. They had all been cut, were bruised or bleeding.

Carroll Cooley's car bounced into the parking lot. The assailants used the distraction of their superior's arrival as an excuse. They faded back into the night.

With the adrenalin of battle depleted, Flynn slid to the ground, his back against his car.

Cooley rushed to him. With Cooley's help, Flynn found residual strength. He forced himself to straighten back up. "That the best they can do? This what happens when a citizen stands up to them?" Flynn asked Cooley. Cooley was genuinely sorry. "I never wanted it to come to this."

"You're too late, Carroll. You're on the wrong side of history."

"Don't you understand? We're all they have."

"Who? The wealthy and well-connected?"

"The poor are mostly victimized by the poor." Cooley yearned to argue his side of it, "Most of my manpower goes to protect the working-class neighborhoods. Just because some shiny suit shows up and tells us we're doing it all wrong, doesn't mean we have to lose the one great tool at our disposal."

Flynn had the courage of his convictions, "One day science will do the job of your precious confession. And when your officers go into court with one, it will stand."

Flynn used his shirt sleeve to wipe the blood off his face, "They'll all be protected. Only now it will be on an even playing field."

"Like hell."

"Don't you want to do more than just send someone to prison? Don't you want to send the right someone?"

"We had the right someone. Miranda was as guilty as sin. You've made the job harder."

"If it's gonna work for the best of us, it's got to work for the least.

Cooley agreed with just a twinge of sarcasm, "Well, you had that part right."

"Miranda is the best thing that ever happened to police work. Scientific fact. Corroborated evidence."

Cooley hesitated. He seemed uncomfortable with what he was about to say, "Jordan Miracle came in with his lawyer. That's ... uh, Johnston's roommate. He ... uh ... confessed to hitting Johnston with a metal lamp. We ... umm ... are going to release Treadaway."

Flynn didn't respond and Cooley started to walk away. After only a few feet, he turned back to face Flynn, "You ... you ... did good, John.

• • •

CHAPTER SIXTY-TWO

DEMON EXPUNGED

John Flynn stood in front of the bathroom mirror in his office washing the blood from his face. He had received a nasty cut on his forehead. His ribs ached. He had gotten a little too old for that kind of action. Any hope of just going home and sleeping was down the drain.

He heard the elevator doors. They had opened and he reluctantly braced for another assault.

He was relieved when he discovered it was Marguerite. "Hey," he greeted her.

"I heard it on the police radio. God, look at you. You okay?" she asked maternally.

Flynn shrugged bravely, "I guess, I'll live."

She continued into the office. They sat across the desk from one another. Flynn unwrapped the cellophane on his third pack of cigarettes that day.

"What are you doing out at this hour?" he asked her.

"Couldn't sleep. When I can't sleep, I research. I guess It's my security blanket."

Flynn smiled, "Anything interesting?"

Marguerite nodded in the affirmative, "Actually, yes..."

Flynn waited.

"You know ... its funny what you can see when you really look," Marguerite continued.

Flynn nodded his agreement, "What is it that caught your eye?"

Marguerite locked her eyes on his, "Something that happened a long time ago."

She hesitated, as if fighting second thoughts. But she was too far to turn back, "A man came home from work and found his wife making love to another man on the commode in their bathroom. The man ran into the bedroom, got a gun from the dresser and came back in firing. The boyfriend made it out the window, but the wife was killed."

Marguerite bobbed her head, agreeing in advance with what she was about to say, "Pretty much an open and shut crime of passion. Voluntary manslaughter." She paused for a second, "Only when the Coroner examined her body, they found what appeared to be a stab wound under her left arm … and that changed everything."

Not sure of where she was going with that story, but understanding the legal logic, Flynn nodded in agreement.

Marguerite continued, "The young prosecutor had the defendant in the interrogation room. 'Did you stab her and then shoot her or did you shoot her first?' It went like that for the better part of twelve hours. Finally, the Defendant, exhausted and alone said: 'I shot her. When she didn't die, I went and got a knife and stabbed her.'"

Flynn's expression turned somber, he recognized that story.

"The young prosecutor was elated. It was exactly what he wanted to hear…. The only problem was…" Her eyes bored into his, "It wasn't the truth. The stab wound under her arm was really the exit wound of the bullet." The young prosecutor had gotten someone to admit to something they had not done.

Flynn sat silent.

Marguerite look straight at him, "Prosecutor John Flynn."

Flynn did not respond, just continued to stare.

Marguerite had finished what she had to say.

Flynn remained motionless.

Marguerite sought to fill the silent void, "Well," she said, "Guess I'll be running along. Maybe now, at least, one of us can get some sleep."

Marguerite left.

Flynn sat stoically reflecting on the dark stain in an impeccable past and lit another cigarette.

* * *

CHAPTER SIXTY-THREE

MIRANDA'S RETRIAL

February 15, 1967

It was the morning of Miranda's retrial. Marguerite waited on a bench across from the Maricopa County Courthouse for John Flynn to arrive. She was immaculately dressed for court. She wore a smart blue ensemble, skirt and jacket over a white blouse. Her hair was perfectly in place.

The morning daily newspaper rested on her lap. Its headline screamed, "Roommate Confesses To Campus Quarterback Killing: Daniel Treadaway Released."

Flynn arrived, confident and conclusive.

Marguerite seemed newly resolute as she showed him the newspaper. She straightened her posture as she stood.

Together, they walked up the steps to the courthouse. Marguerite walked with him, step-for-step, with a renewed sense of purpose.

The trial dragged on for eight boring days. Every piece of evidence and witness the prosecutor produced, Flynn argued against as inadmissible in light of the Supreme Court decision.

On the eighth day, with the prosecutor seeming to have run out of material, Flynn turned to him and said, "What are we messing around for? Let's send him home."

Flynn asked permission to approach the bench, "Your Honor, may we approach?"

Flynn was confident they had won.

As they approached the judge, the prosecutor surprised Flynn, "I have one more witness, your Honor," the prosecutor asserted.

"And who might that be," asked the judge, bored to the point of lethargy.

"Twila Hoffman, your Honor," came the response.

Although he had long anticipated it, Flynn feigned outrage. "We've not been informed, your Honor," Flynn protested vociferously.

The judge looked sheepishly at Flynn.

"Well, you know, John. That happens. Someone reads something in the paper and it jogs their memory. They come forward. I'm going to allow it."

That was the end for Miranda and Flynn knew it. Twila was a totally incredible witness but they would have to believe her if they wanted to convict him. And one look at the jury and Flynn knew they wanted to do that.

Miranda knew it too.

Still, as was his way, Flynn tried his hardest. He tore into Twila. He confronted every lie she told. But just as Paul Lewis had anticipated, she had been thoroughly coached. Twila repeated Miranda's original confession, word-for-word. She even spoke the part where he supposedly said, "I put it in one inch."

The jury deliberated for only a short time.

"Guilty as charged," came the verdict.

Miranda stood to hear his sentence. Judge Wren ran the charges and sentences together, laying one on top of the other. The practical impact was, with time served and time off for good behavior, Miranda would only be away for a relatively short time.

Miranda waited for the court officers to come and cuff him. They would take him back to jail immediately.

As he waited, Judge Wren came down off the bench and approached. "Mister Miranda," he began, as he extended his hand, "It was an honor to have had you in my court," he declared.

They shook hands. The judge nodded to Flynn and left.

Miranda looked at Flynn, more than a little surprised by the judge's reaction. Flynn just shrugged in incredulity.

"An honor to have had me in his court," Miranda paraphrased the judge's pronouncement to Flynn.

Flynn could only smirk and nod.

"And that's something ... right?" Miranda asked, seeking reassurance.

Flynn replied, compassionately, "Oh, you bet."

CHAPTER SIXTY-FOUR

THE TRAIL ABOVE CAREFREE

The words of a young rake in the district attorney's office came roaring back. It was from a time when all the young men thought about were pretty women and career advancement: "When your ship comes in, just be sure you're not standing at the airport." That glib line that had been but a throwaway then, now had real resonance.

Flynn had been to the mountain, the pinnacle of his legal career. He had achieved financial success and national recognition. And yet was living alone, away from the only people that really mattered, that gave his life its real meaning.

What could it feel like to be with one more woman? He had been with many but they brought him no solace, no joy, nothing other than momentary and, ultimately elusive, satisfaction.

He had succeeded on the grandest stage, yet it brought him no sense of grandeur.

The foolish man storms the court and demands satisfaction.

The humble man approaches the judge and asks for mercy.

"Pride cometh before the fall." The voice of his lord and savior, long forgotten, now called out to Flynn, "Be not like Lucifer storming the court of God."

He waited for her on the path that curved up into the hills above Carefree. He watched the sun slide behind the majestic cliffs of the Tonto Mountains. He was mindful of the hour, the hour when basking rattle snakes slithered homeward, wary of larger predators.

As the pastels of dusk began to leak through, Camille and Chester descended around a corner on the trail. They stopped. As if by instinct Chester became agitated. He swung his head from side to side and pawed the ground as if to warn Flynn not to come any closer. Camille petted his neck in a calming gesture of reassurance.

Chester settled.

They looked at each other, neither speaking, the missing piece of each other's life.

After a minute, Camille loosened the reins and Chester began to move slowly forward.

Flynn fell into step at her heels.

Together, they finished the journey along the trail above Carefree.

* * *

CHAPTER SIXTY-FIVE

Amapola Reprise

Phoenix, Arizona, January 1976

Police Officer Doren Buhlheiser was only a block from the Amapola when the call came in. He activated his patrol car's lights and sirens and sped toward the cafe. Misjudging his approach, Buhlheiser bounced the police car onto the sidewalk.

The two chicanos were just running out and slammed into the incoming patrol car. The force knocked them back into the cantina.

Buhlheiser and his partner jumped out preparing to restrain the suspects. But Fernando and Eduardo were not about to go peacefully.

The younger office, Jerry Rivers, tried to grab Eduardo in a headlock.

Buhlheiser wrenched Fernando's arm behind him in order to cuff him.

Eduardo slithered out of the headlock and pushed Rivers back. Rivers got just enough of Eduardo's shirt to keep him from getting away. Eduardo slipped and fell. He pulled Rivers to the floor with him. The two men wrestled around in the sawdust.

Buhlheiser managed to pin Fernando up against the wall but needed both hands to restrain him and could not reach his own handcuffs.

Mary Lou had come out from behind the bar carrying several dish rags. She stuffed them under Miranda's shirt in an attempt to staunch the bleeding. She tried to concentrate amidst the chaos. Mary Lou looked up, "He's … he's … dying."

Buhlhesier made the mistake of turning his head toward Mary Lou.

"Get a god damn ambulance in here," he bellowed.

The momentary distraction allowed Fernando to thrust back into Buhlheiser, pushing him away. Fernando turned and tried to reach for Buhlheiser's gun.

"No, you don't, you son of a bitch."

Buhlheiser lunged at Fernando and drove both of them across a table. More glass shattered, more wooden tables broke.

Rivers had pinned Eduardo, face down, onto the floor. He had succeeded in cuffing one wrist but was struggling to secure the other. In frustration, he drove Eduardo's face into the floor over and over again.

"Quit strugglin', god damn it!"

A foot away, Buhlhesier finally had Fernando pinned. The older officer had placed his forearm across Fernando's neck as a restraint. He had the suspect pinned to the floor. Fernando's face was turning red as he struggled to breathe. Rivers finally managed to cuff Eduardo.

Buhlhesier searched his own pockets for an admonition card. Chest heaving from exertion, temper shortening from frustration, he turned towards his partner.

"Read'em."

Rivers was still dealing with Eduardo who continued to struggle.

"I can't get to my card," he yelled to his partner.

"Habla ingles, asshole?" Buhlhesier asked Fernando angrily.

"No."

Buhlheiser hauled Fernando to his feet and shook him, "Ta hell with all of it.... Let's go, asshole."

On the bloody floor of the Amapola Café, Ernesto Miranda's life was ebbing away in the sawdust. Panicked that he would die as a "John Doe," Mary Lou frantically rifled his pockets for some identification, a wallet, a green card, anything.

Her hand brushed against a Miranda card in his pants pocket. She withdrew it and held it up towards Doren Buhlhesier. He was almost at the door with his handcuffed prisoner.

"Wait," Mary Lou called, "Here."

Buhlheiser struggled his detainee back within arm's length of Mary Lou. He took the card from her outstretched hand.

Recognizing what it was he started to read: "You have the right to remain silent. Anything you say can be used against you in a court of Law. You have the right to the presence of an attorney to assist you prior to questioning and to be with you during questioning, if you so desire. If you cannot afford an attorney you have the right to have an attorney appointed for you prior to questioning."

They were the words codified by the United States Supreme Court, known as "the Miranda Rights." Rights won for them in the name of the man they had just killed.

Satisfied he had fulfilled his legal obligation, Buhlheiser shoved his prisoner out the door.

Mary Lou knelt beside Miranda.

She placed her hand on his chest ... and began to pray for him.

* * *

EPILOGUE

It was the bottom of the sixth of Scottie's championship game. His team led three-to-two.

Rex Lee became Solicitor General of the United States during the Reagan Administration.

Scottie wound up and threw towards home. The pitch caught the outside corner.

The umpire hollered, "Stee-rike."

Scottie tried to relax. He rubbed dirt on the ball stalling for time, quieting his nerves.

Carroll Cooley became Captain of the "Crimes Against Persons" division of the Phoenix Police Department.

Scottie reared back and threw with all his might towards home.

The batter swung and missed.

"Strike Twooo."

Scottie looked over towards the stands. His father, John Flynn, was standing at the top of the bleachers, in the last row.

Scottie straightened just a little. A calm came over him.

In the wake of "Miranda," The American Bar Association formed a committee dedicated to criminal procedures and minimal justice standards. John Flynn, was accepted to the Burger Commission, and played an integral part in the creation of "The Criminal Code." It is today in place in all fifty states.

Scottie threw again.

The batter swung again and missed.

Gloves were thrown to the ground.

Caps were tossed into the air.

His teammates ran to Scottie and hugged him and kissed him and tousled his hair.

Arizona was the first state to adopt it.

APPENDIX A

INTERVIEW WITH JOHN FLYNN

On Labor Day weekend 1979, Joe Wallenstein flew to Arizona to meet with John Flynn at his law offices in Phoenix and later continued the discussion at his pecan ranch in Gilbert.

Over the course of three days, they spoke extensively about Flynn's life and the various aspects of Miranda. What follows is a transcript of the recorded portion of their conversation.

Flynn shared previously unreported details and insights, offering a rare glimpse into the human side of his story. When they parted, tentative plans were made to see each other again to continue their conversation. That next meeting, however, was not destined to be. John Flynn died suddenly and unexpectedly three months later reaching for an unopened pack of cigarettes beneath the front seat of his Porsche.

Wallenstein: Can you tell us a little about yourself, background material? Native of Arizona?

Flynn: I was born and raised in Arizona, Tortilla Flats, as a matter of fact, a little place in the hills out here. Educated in Phoenix – Joined the Marine Corp when I was 17. Three years in the South Pacific in the Marine Corp. Came back, started mid-term at the University of Arizona in 1946. Went to school 3 1/2 years and got my law degree. Came out and took court appointments [indigent defendants] – became a member of the Maricopa County Attorney's Office which is the District Attorney's Office. Prosecutor about 2 1/2 years. We were like gang busters – young and enthusiastic – clean up the town and that sort of thing. Went into private practice law – specialized in litigation, trial of cases, probably 40% criminal cases and 60% civil cases. Joined with a group of other young fellows – formed a law firm – number of years – left that and became a managing partner in the city's largest law firm – one of the managing partners for about five years. About '59-head of the litigation section – trials of cases. Left that again and formed my own firm for about another six or seven years – down in the bank – all the antiques – big, lush offices – got tired of the whole thing – thought I'd cut back my practice – bought a big house, redwood, over in Fort Bragg – above San Francisco where Mendocino is on the coast. Intended to spend a lot of time there – got very little accomplished. Got this pecan farm and that's about it.

Wallenstein: Your folks also from Arizona?

Flynn: No, my father was from Montana and my mother from Idaho.

NOTE: Joe Wallenstein conducted this interview with the assistance of Bob Stambler.

Stambler: What part of Idaho?

Flynn: Headweser – my grandfather was the first man to ever herd sheep in northern Idaho. They have a mountain named after him – Brundage Mountain – McCall Lake. It's a ski place. All the old homesteads and the sheep camps up there where the family on my mother's side lives. Beautiful country – Riggins on the Salmon River – used to spend all my summers there when I was a boy – it's just gorgeous. We went back this summer – drove back up by the Salmon River as far as the road would go and up over the top to Bergdorf. Still total wilderness country, there's no paved roads or anything – had a four-wheel – tried to get up over it – went to one of the old sheep camps with my grandfather there – still got the corrals – they're tumbled down now and some of the shacks but they're still out in the meadows where they have the sheep in the summer time.

Stambler: You still find a lot of the Basque sheep herders in Idaho.

Flynn: Oh, yeah. His partner was a Basque. Chevarier was my father's partner.

Wallenstein: How did you first become involved with Miranda and the case?

Flynn: Well, at that time I was in that major law firm that I told you about.

Wallensten: What was the name of it?

Flynn: Lewis & Roca was the name of the firm. At the time the American Civil Liberties Union did not have any kind of an office in Arizona, but they had what in smaller communities they called correspondent attorneys. They are an attorney who volunteers his services to review requests for ACLU intervention and Miranda had written to the ACLU and they would divert the letter to this correspondent attorney – what his main problem was that he was in a prison.

Wallenstein: Was that Corcoran? Robert Corcoran?

Flynn: Yeah, and Corcoran as corresponding attorney had polled the bar association asking for volunteers during the course of his tenure. Can I call upon you if I have a case that needs some assistance because obviously he had his own practice and couldn't possibly handle all the cases. So, he called me and I said, well I'll volunteer the firm's litigation section to handle two cases a year and Miranda we one of them.

Wallenstein: Was it a difficult thing to do? Did Miranda get a lot of notoriety? Locally? Or was it only at the point it went to the Supreme Court?

Flynn: Right.

Wallenstein: It was really just another case?

Flynn: Just another case, very routine and he was charged with two different cases. Robbery and Kidnapping and Rape and Kidnapping. And the Rape and Kidnapping case was tried; the jury selection started at 9:00 in the morning and that case was tried and he was convicted by 3:00 in the afternoon. He was sentenced to 20-30. The following day he was tried on the Robbery and Kidnapping case and the same thing – 9:00 in the morning jury selected – 3:00 in the afternoon he's found guilty. He got 20-40 years to run consecutively on the other end of the other one. So, when you say notoriety, you don't get much notoriety out of a one day –

Wallenstein: Well, the reason I was asking, I'm thinking that we're talking about 1963-1966 and my question was going to be: Was it a difficult case from the climate of the community in those days?

Flynn: Not any more than any other rape, kidnapping, or robbery. It wasn't a brutal rape, the girl wasn't really injured at all. I think she was marginally close to being mentally retarded, but it wouldn't be fair to characterize her as mentally retarded, but not really very quick and passive through the whole thing, apparently. Hadn't been injured in any way or harmed. In fact, the reason they caught Miranda was because he came back a second time.

Wallenstein: Didn't the brother spot him cruising the neighborhood?

Flynn: And the brother caught him, partial license plate, cruising the second time. He gave the license number and that's what led them to Miranda. And in his mind I think he thought the girl was not that unhappy and the next time it might not be rape – he just drops by and…. And the robbery and kidnapping, he approached a girl in the parking lot of a bank – she worked for the bank or something – went up to her and said get in the car – they got in the car – had a knife – made some overt sexual suggestions or whatever to her. She ended up giving him her purse with $1.80 or something.

Stambler: John, you say that it all happened between 9:00 in the morning and 3:00 in the afternoon. Why? Was it that cut and dry? Even with someone who, theoretically, doesn't matter to the public, it doesn't normally happen quite that fast, does it?

Flynn: Well, you're talking about a criminal justice system that existed in Arizona and across the country.

Stambler: Was it the minority thing?

Flynn: Sixteen years, okay. Miranda itself, the companion cases – Escobedo, Gideon, Matt vs. Ohio, the search and seizure case, you have all of those occurring in that time frame of six or seven years of the Warren Court. That changed the criminal justice system – those things don't happen anymore. They have built into the system and established procedures that you're not going to have a trial like that. It would be almost impossible to have a trial like that.

Stambler: Was it more so because of Miranda being a Chicano, do you think? At that time?

Flynn: I don't think so, we had a system then. We didn't have public defenders and all of that's occurred, subsequent to these cases. We had either young lawyers who were just out of law school, that's the way I started, signed a list and you got $1550 bucks to represent a guy or you had older lawyers who basically, perhaps, shouldn't have been practicing law, but they'd been practicing 20-30 years and they would get on the list. The whole thing was rather perfunctory, you did what you could do, you didn't have any disclosure, couldn't file a motion to suppress evidence, Matt hadn't been decided. There was no question about the admissibility of a confession. They have a confession, they have an eyewitness, they have the whole thing. The underlying facts of Miranda, had they known them at the time and had there been a criminal justice system that required the prosecution to reveal all of its evidence and give it to the defense counsel, it never would have occurred. When the case came back for re-trial Matt vs. Ohio has been decided, Miranda has been decided so we're entitled now to evidentiary hearings and to require the prosecution to produce all of that evidence that never had been produced the first time. We found all kind of things. For example: The way the confession came about they had brought the girl down to the courthouse and put Miranda in a line-up with several other individuals and the girl had walked in and she wasn't able to identify anybody. Okay. They take Miranda back to the interrogation room and he walks in the door, turns around to the detective and says, "how did I do"? And the guy looks him in the eye and says, "you flunked."

They then bring the girl in and as she walks through the door, Miranda looks up at her and says, "that's her." That's the end of that stunt. That's the way the case really happened. And in the subsequent trial she was not permitted to make an in-court identification for the reason that she had not identified him in the line-up, the subsequent identification was tainted by the one-on-one confrontation and under recent Supreme Court cases you can't do that. So, Miranda would never have been convicted in the first instance had the criminal justice system required the prosecution to deliver all that evidence to the defense counsel. So, an interesting aspect of it is that Miranda as part of the whole series of cases creates a requirement that never would have permitted Miranda to be convicted in the first place.

Wallenstein: And, in fact, the safeguards that occurred in the first trial protected him in the second. In a way he was the forerunner of his own defense later on.

Flynn: Precisely.

Wallenstein: Let me back-track a second because it is fascinating and I hate to break it up, but Alvin Moore? The papers made reference to the fact that he had not practiced law for 12-16 years. Is that accurate?

Flynn: Alvin was practicing law when I started and as far as I knew was still practicing but he was at the twilight of his practice and was taking court appointments.

Wallenstein: But as you said before, young guys did it, older guys did it, it was the natural progression the older guy's turn came up and he took it.

Flynn: Right.

Stambler: Well, his indication then, no, his inference, was really that if Miranda had not been a Chicano and travelled in a Mormon community and the girl had not been a blonde; that was one of Moore's statements, does that have any validity?

Flynn: I totally disagree with that. They had cold evidence. The girl comes in and that's him. Okay? And they got a confession. About which there was no suggestion that the confession had been coerced or he was forced to give the confession – in the traditional sense of it being voluntary it was clearly voluntary. He sat down and wrote it out. They helped him write it out because you don't say, "well, I put it in that far." Miranda is not that articulate or was not certainly at that time articulate to have been that refined but they had a Patricia's Law case and what was his defense?

Wallenstein: And that was fairly standard, I mean it was not at all unusual. Confession was one of the bulwarks

Flynn: Right. That's why the case was so rapid. As I recall they called the girl and they called the police officer and what else do you need? Now it's up to you Miranda, explain yourself out of it. And there was no way he could explain himself out of it.

Wallenstein: Did he not at one time ask to be represented but at that time in a preliminary hearing you didn't have to be represented? You see our information, basically is coming from other journalists and they kind of take their own license sometimes. So if our information…

Flynn: Now that comes about at a later time again as a consequence of the collection of cases. When he was first arrested, and that was another thing, he confessed to the second crime, robbery and kidnapping based on a statement by the police officer that, "Look, you're caught, might as well get everything cleared up, can't be in any worse trouble than you are, what about this robbery-kidnapping case?" And they brought that girl down and she did identify him in the robbery-kidnapping. And, you know, hard on him, which led him to believe they were going to file against him so he confessed to that. It was the second confession robbery and kidnapping.

So, when he went before the magistrate in the preliminary hearing he now finds two cases and he's unhappy. Because in his mind at least it was represented to him that they weren't going to do this second one to him. That's when he starts asking for an attorney of the magistrate and the magistrate says, "I have no authority to appoint counsel to you at this stage of the proceeding." Of course, that's not the law anymore either. They're required to appoint you assistance and "you can't have a lawyer" – that became a large factor in his second trial after the reversal by the Supreme Court. For the reason, that the only reason that he was convicted the second time was because they came forth with a new witness and that's the common-law wife, who now pops up in jail and here's Miranda. He's been down in front of the judge. The judge says, "you can't have a lawyer, no way you can have a lawyer." Here is the only person he can ask for help is this common-law wife and according to her, womanly curiosity being what it is, says to him, "What did you do?" He now proceeds, classically, to confess to her exactly how the confession reads even to the "half inch." So we moved to suppress that confession on the basis that they had deprived him of the right to counsel, and he was up there attempting to get somebody to help him. They put him in the position. He was arrested without probable cause, denied him the right to counsel and now they want to utilize his confession from a situation which they have wrongfully created by having him in jail. But we failed.

Wallenstein: You tried, did you not, to discredit her for other reasons. She was an incredible witness.

Flynn: Oh, yes.

Wallenstein: She had falsified public documents.

Flynn: Right. All kinds of things.

Wallenstein: Do you think she was being used...

Flynn: Oh, I have no doubt in my mind that she was being used and whether or not she had any assistance from the prosecutor in helping her with her story about how he confessed and the "half inch" I don't know. But by that point in time I think six years had passed. They had a child together. She had visited him in prison up to a point in time. After a couple of years she came down and he said, "I understand you're sleeping with someone else." She apparently figured he was saying, "I'm gonna get the child when I get out." And so he had created for himself a situation where she did not want him out of that prison, ever, ever, ever. So she had all the motivation in the world.

Wallenstein: I've always wondered about that. Why?

Flynn: That's why she came forth. I mean she had all the motivation in the world.

Stambler: That's what we were conjecturing about last night.

Flynn: But we had the case. The second time around we had suppressed all the evidence that they had obtained. We had suppressed her in-court identification, she couldn't identify him. The Supreme Court has suppressed the confession. They're just totally emasculated, they don't have a case. This is like Friday evening and I turned to the prosecutor and I was real happy you know and I said what are we messing around for – lets send him home. He says, "Well, I may have to, but I think I got one more witness" and lo and behold it was Twila. The common-law wife. New confession. Bearing in mind the case has now lasted nine days and eight of it have been in out-of-court hearings suppressing minor evidence. I think that the jury at that point in time began to sense and there was a lot of publicity, newspaper people around who ordinarily wouldn't be here and I think they identified Miranda. I think by the time that the case went to the jury they knew who they were dealing with and what it was all about. They had made the nexus in their mind to the case, the publicity and the defendant in this case. While her testimony was weak and discredited and all the rest of it, the nine days and all the legal wrangling they had come to the conclusion that this was Ernesto Miranda.

Wallenstein: So, it's funny the public opinion caught up with him the second time not the first.

Flynn: That's right.

Wallenstein: But wouldn't her confession have been inadmissible since the prosecuting attorneys had not submitted it originally under the ruling that you had to bring forth all the evidence?

Flynn: We still did not have at the time of the second trial our new rules of criminal procedure and, of course, there is still the exception of surprise. I mean it's not uncommon in the trying of a case that someone reads something in a newspaper and comes forth. We still have it happen frequently. We'll get a telephone call in the middle of a case and someone will say, "Hey, you know, I know something about that." And if you can demonstrate that you are, in fact, surprised and you just now became aware of it the court will still permit.

Stambler: So, in other words you can still avoid the sharing of the information with the prosecution, that's the loophole.

Flynn: Yeah. If you convince the judge.

Wallenstein: There were four cases that were tried. Were there not? Or that were brought together as one that came to be known as Miranda. Vigneros, Westover and Stewart?

Flynn: Yeah.

Wallenstein: They were all represented under the banner of Miranda?

Flynn: Right. The only reason the case was called Miranda was because his was the first number on the docket.

Wallenstein: That's also fascinating to me, because he was essentially an anonymous guy until that hand of fate plucked him out or whatever.

Stambler: That was an interesting thing too, I mean you know, as Joe said, "We haven't talked to the man who was there, but by newspaper accounts when they're talking about the Supreme Court that day with the Sam Shepard thing preceding you on the docket, it seems like it's so dramatic and so theatrical it's incredible. And, of course, the version in the paper was this bright attorney in awe of what was going on with F. Lee Bailey up there and not knowing if he could be as good as F. Lee Bailey. I mean dramatically, it's beautiful, but it's kind of like a press agent's dream.

Wallenstein: It must have been kind of awesome.

Flynn: It was. And, of course, it was Bailey's first shot, his first emergence on the horizon. I never heard of F. Lee Bailey and neither had anybody else heard of F. Lee Bailey until the Sam Sheppard case. That was the case that propelled him to whatever he has attained.

Wallenstein: Yeah, media fame.

Flynn: Well, Lee is a friend of mine. Came to know him after that. We participated in cases from time to time.

Wallenstein: The papers made reference to the fact that some of the other attorneys wanted to argue the sixth amendment and that you clung to the fifth, you thought it would be the fifth amendment.

Flynn: Yeah, what happened is that when the case came into the office, there were a group of us, five of us. What we did is we went downstairs to another law firm and there was a fellow who is now a Professor at the University of Utah Law School by the name of Rex Lee. Rex had just left the Supreme Court, there as Justice Black's law clerk. In our office was another lawyer, John Frank. John had been Justice Black's law clerk back in earlier days. Probably the 40's or 50's, around there. And he was an excellent appellate lawyer, that was his specialty. He was the appellate lawyer in the law firm and I was the litigation.

We went down to see Rex Lee. It was simply for guidance and for a feeling. We told him what the problem, you know, what the issue was, what the court's inclination would be. You know, this thing had been hammered at a thousand times in preceding years, you know, what were a defendant's rights. Rex said, "Well, from my observation of the court having been with Justice Black, conferences, hearings and everything that was going on around the court the time is right. You've got a real issue. It's something that the court might really be interested in. The time has come, they're going to take hold of something like this. Which was encouraging, you know, but the percentages of having a review granted by the United States Supreme Court were one in a thousand. So, we went back and sat down and drafted a petition and we drafted it in the strongest possible light. The trick to the petition of service was to hit the court in maybe three or four pages of dynamite. Like, you know, shock their conscience and get them. So, that's why it starts out "indigent defendant," "mentally defective," all of it, you know, wake 'em up, sort of technique which was John Frank's thought. He knew what would intrigue the court.

So, we filed a petition setting forth the basic facts of what had occurred. And never really expecting that they would grant a review. We just expected to get back: "Review Denied." Instead it came back: "We have accepted Review." That's the big step when you can get them to even listen to it. Then we sat down and had a conference, John Frank and myself and three other fellows. We went round and round, how do we approach this? We pulled every case ever written on the subject.

The forerunner, of course, was Escobedo. But that was a sixth amendment, right to counsel case. And the question was, you know, was this right to counsel, was the focus on whether or not trying to persuade the court because you can't even get a confession now unless the lawyer's there. Or is there something more to it? So we went round and round. There's a whole series of cases – different aspects of this that the court refused the very thing that we were going to be asking. So we ended up on how we were going to structure the brief and what the focus would be and what our position would be and an argument over whether it should be a fifth amendment argument or a sixth amendment argument. And myself and one of the other fellows felt it should be a fifth amendment argument, John and the other two fellows felt it should be a sixth amendment argument. And that argument between us never stopped. Which in the long run was very helpful to me because my mind was into the fifth amendment part of the argument and I was mentally prepared for that. And, Justice Black the first shot out of the box, I hadn't been on my feet two seconds, and he said, "Well, Mr. Flynn isn't it really the Fifth Amendment." I was ready for it, see.

Wallenstein: What was that moment like? Did you know you were in good shape?

Flynn: Well, I didn't know if I was in good shape, but I knew I could respond. But, you have to appreciate the argument, it's not what you would call anything persuasive. It would be a total mistake to even suggest that I could take any credit for the decision. Purely, it was a consequence of the argument. I had started to outline my argument when Black made that statement. I said, "Well, yes" and started to expound on it a little bit and I was interrupted by Justice White. White took the real pragmatic approach which we feared the most. He said, "Mr. Flynn, was this confession voluntary or involuntary?" That's a very difficult question. It certainly wasn't involuntary with the sense that anyone was standing with a gun at his head or beating him with a lead pipe or lights or anything of that kind. "So, how is it involuntary?" So, I'm saying, "Well, it's involuntary." "How is it involuntary?" Pressing me for an answer. I'm trying to articulate well, it's involuntary because he's in the police station, the police are there and the rest of it, he doesn't know etc."

"I didn't ask you that. Was it voluntary or involuntary?" He was just impaling me and finally Justice Black came to the rescue and he said, "Well, Mr. Flynn isn't it involuntary because..." and he began to rescue me. And no sooner had he finished expounding in essence a position on that when Potter Stewart grabbed the spotlight and he starts in on a long hypothetical question, "Well, aren't you suggesting that to be a policeman in a police station etc., etc., etc.," and it seemed to me like he talked for five minutes and I got one word out of my mouth about "no," when Justice Fortas intervened and proceeds for another five minutes to expound his view in contradiction to Justice Stewart. And it ended up after about fifteen minutes of Justice Stewart turning to the Chief Justice and saying, "Chief Justice, I think it's unfair to Mr. Flynn in the presentment of his agreement that Justice Fortas and I having been using him to exchange our views. I would recommend to the Chief Justice that he be allowed additional time if he wants it." Well, you know, at that point I didn't want any additional time. I just wanted to be the hell out of there. So the exchange went back and forth and I think I talked for about another five or six minutes. And the yellow light went on. You know how the thing works don't you? You're very carefully structured. They've got lights next to the podium. Green light, yellow light, red light. And when the green light is on you talk. When the yellow light is on, you have sixty seconds and you're told once if not a hundred times when the red light comes on if you're in the middle of a word, you quit. So the yellow light came around, I thanked the court and sat down.

So the point I make is they had their thoughts. You have to understand that. Those are really profound men up there. You may disagree with their philosophical approach to problems, but I don't think anyone could discredit them in any way for not knowing everything. They probably know as much or more about your case than you do. They have read everything. The Sheppard case was a classic example. The brief and the transcripts in the Sheppard case must have been that high; the documents. And Bailey argued his case. And the podium is here, and the appellant is here and the appellee is over here. And the person next to the podium is supposed to argue. There was a young assistant attorney general from the State of Ohio sitting next to the podium who everybody felt was going to argue the case. Next to him was Saxby. William Saxby, the Senator who was then the Attorney General, later to become the Senator.

Bailey sits down and the young fellow starts to get up like this and Saxby reaches over and puts his hand on his shoulder and he stands up because he sees an opportunity to be on stage and indeed some of the Kennedys were there. They were admitting them as was the practice and the courtroom was packed and it was a big day. He proceeds to get up and says, "This case reminds me of another Sacco and Vanzetti." And Black comes up out of his chair and said, "I hope we're not going to try that case today." He'd been on the court back in the Sacco/Vanzetti days. He (Saxby) then says, "Well, then whatever it was, something in the record, writ of habeas corpus, we weren't even represented. The attorney general's office didn't even have notice of Mr. Bailey's petition." And it seems to me it was Potter Stewart said, "Would you repeat that Mr. Saxby?' He said, "We weren't even allowed, we weren't even noticed that the hearing on writ of habeas corpus was going before the district court." He (Stewart) reached down and grabbed one of these massive volumes and turned the pages and said, "Just a minute. I refer you to page one-forty-one of the transcript at which it says, Mr. F.

Lee Bailey moved the admission of the Assistant Attorney General of the State of Ohio to be allowed to practice in the Federal District Court at the hearing on ..." How do you answer that? They proceeded to emasculate him. I mean he didn't know the record, he wasn't prepared, they just tore him to bits, just made a complete fool out of him. But it demonstrates that they just know everything and that's why I come back to the position that positions are taken ...

[Flynn is interrupted by phone call here]

That's why I say I think you know any focus you try to put on counsel coming up with a brilliant argument persuading the Supreme Court – that might be great for writing but it's not factually sound. I think we did an excellent job in focusing on the problem and getting it through. And the reason that I argued the case instead of John Frank who is truly an appellate lawyer, he specializes in appeals, was that it was his judgment that the court would be more interested in my practical knowledge of the working of the police department and that it would be of assistance to the court to let them really know what happens in a police station because they do live in an ivory tower. Now they may know the record and they may know the law, they're brilliant but few of them have had the practical experience of knowing what happens in a police department. I mean being down on the street and in the room where the interrogation takes place. What is the impact on the individual? What is the atmosphere? And so the only contribution I could really make and which I attempted to make was to paint for them a picture of what goes on inside a police interrogation room and what happens to an indigent Mexican Chicano who's brought there with two big guys with guns on their hip, in a room and set down and they wanna ask him questions. And is he responding voluntarily because he just wants to get it off his chest or is he doing it because he is in total awe and fear of the police department, the setting and the atmosphere. Shouldn't he be reminded that he has rights. The right to have a lawyer there, the right to have assistance from his own government through these times. So that's probably all I could say about the contribution I made to it was to tell them what it was really like down there.

Wallenstein: Was there a transcript of that day? Would that be part of the police record?

Flynn: Well, they had recording a thing there. I never made any attempt to get it.

Wallenstein: It would be interesting to have.

Flynn: I know they recorded it, whether or not they prepared a report of the recording, I don't know. Unless there was some special reason to transcribe the recording I would imagine they are not transcribed. And I would wonder if after a passage of time if they don't just reuse the tape. Because you're at the court of last resort. It's not like you're going to go somewhere else and need a transcript unless for some reason somebody missed something and one of the Justices said, "Hey, I'd like to have that typed up so I can review it again."

Wallenstein: You were about forty years old at the time? Were they worried about a young man approaching the court; a young upstart?

Flynn: I think Bailey was younger than I was. I think he was 33 at the time.

Wallenstein: Who were all the guys? There was John Frank, yourself. Can you tell me who else?

Flynn: Rex Lee.

Wallenstein: You said there were five guys from your office.

Flynn: Well, let's see there was Bob Geneson, Paul Ulrich and Roger Kaufman were the other three.

Wallenstein: You know I was always under the impression because these other fellows Stewart, Vigneros – one was from New York.

Flynn: Well, they all had lawyers. You see this agreement in the so-called Miranda case became a national case. The National Association of Attorneys General applied for the right to intervene as Amicus, as a friend of the court to file a brief, and they did. The National American Civil Liberties Union applied for and got the permission to file an Amicus brief to argue and they were permitted and did. Vigneros had an attorney. The Attorney General from the State of New York appeared. Westover had an attorney. The Solicitor General appeared on behalf of the United States Government. Stewart had an attorney. The Attorney General of the State of California appeared. They all appeared and argued. The whole thing extended over two days. It started late in the morning after Sheppard, carried through the rest of that day into the next morning before all the arguments of the so-called Miranda case were presented. You had a whole army of lawyers arguing the case. There were little different twists in the other cases. See, they weren't all identical. One was a Federal case. Each one had distinguishing features and they were trying to cover a whole area of police interrogation in different settings so they could solve a whole multitude of problems.

Stambler: Were there considerable similarities?

Flynn: Well, they all involved confessions.

Stambler: In terms of the police department?

Flynn: Yes. In the course of an interrogation.

Stambler: In other words it was that same thing, the fright or whatever.

Flynn: In essence. One was a prolonged in-custody. The guy was in custody, I forget which one it was, for a substantial period of time. Miranda had not been in custody long. It was different aspects of the situation we were trying to cover and they used Miranda, being the number one case, but they also used Miranda to express the whole setting. Then they tied the others in bits and pieces to Miranda.

Wallenstein: Would it be accurate to say that it was your area of knowing the nuts and bolts of police procedure that was one of the things

Flynn: I think that was one of the things they were most interested in. In other words, the Solicitor General was arguing, "What Mr. Flynn had said and the others have said the FBI does anyway, we've always warned them of their rights, you don't need to impose that kind of sanctions on the FBI, the FBI has for fifty years warned everybody that they have this, and this, and this."

Wallenstein: Efrem Zimbalist, Jr. wouldn't lie.

Flynn: Right.

Stambler: You were the first man up to bat though, right?

Flynn: Right.

Wallenstein: You know, you would think that because it did lead to a Supreme Court decision there would be some documentation of the works over a period of two days.

Flynn: Yeah.

Wallenstein: I get the impression in talking that things started rather slowly as a routine case, took on more importance, but in terms of the public perception it really peaked and became bigger than life at the point of the re-trial. At that point there was press, notoriety and it was already in the Supreme Court. Were you ever under any sort of personal pressure? The reason I ask you this is because in the course of our work we come in contact with a great number of police officers and I remember going back several years, that Miranda to them was the kiss of death. It was the end of the world. Now, in fact, it appears if anything Miranda moved police work away from confessions into much more scientific areas.

Flynn: Exactly. It's the greatest thing that ever happened to the police department.

Wallenstein: But at the time they thought it was...

Flynn: Absolutely.

Stambler: But, John, don't you think that a lot of that was that you were hearing from the old-timers and that was the only way they knew how to operate? They had been operating that way for so long in terms of the intimidation of prisoners.

Flynn: It was the easiest way. I mean, you know, get a guy down in the room and sweat him and get him to tell you all the facts and get him to tell you all the details and tell you where he hid the gun and this and this. And you just walk out and get it and the case is over.

Wallenstein: Miranda really brought it into the 20th Century. Voice prints, fingerprints, forensics.

Flynn: Exactly.

Stambler: You know it's strange because my dad was on the LAPD and I can remember when it happened he said, "that's it, I've got 25 years in, I was going to go to 30. I think I'm going to retire because I'll never be able to work under these conditions." It was kind of vague and, of course, you get that one-sided explanation, but then when you hear the stories of how they got confessions back in the old days. Hanging a guy off a bridge and starting to untie his shoelaces and they're holding him by his shoes. The total intimidation, the fear, the whole works. In many cases I'm sure they were guilty but in many cases they were innocent but just scared.

Flynn: Well, I had a personal experience when I was prosecuting attorney. I got a confession out of a guy for something he didn't do. Wasn't a confession of a crime, nobody questioned there was a crime but it was how he committed that crime and after six or seven hours of interrogation in the police station I got him to admit to something he didn't do. So it can happen. And I wasn't beating him or anything, I was just taking him back and back and back and back and "I don't believe you." Now look you claim you're telling me the truth, you're not telling me the truth and just pounding and pounding and pounding. He just gave up and admitted it. Much to my chagrin I found out before the trial of the case that what I had forced him to admit, in fact, hadn't happened. He had come into his house and his wife was sitting nude on the commode with her boyfriend. He went and got a gun and shot her. You know, pretty classically a manslaughter case. So they've got the body down in the morgue and we get a call from the medical examiner that in addition to a bullet hole there appears to be a stab wound under her left armpit. Well, now that changed the whole context. The guy's telling us a story that he found his wife nude on the commode with her boyfriend and he shot her. Well, when did he stab her? So where's the knife? And so I'm after him. There wasn't any knife.

Wallenstein: Given the notoriety and the media, the early police reaction, did that put a strain on you and your work relationship with police? Were you then the guy who had opened Pandora's Box and turned loose this incredible demon?

Flynn: I don't think so. Phoenix is or was a relatively small community and over the years I got to know a lot of policemen and police associations and had been an assistant prosecuting attorney. I think they had the same reaction all police officers did. That it was just an impossible requirement. All the criminals were going to go free, ridiculous, etc. etc. But I started doing a lot of lecturing to police departments and policemen and took the very position that you suggest. And that is that it was going to require them to upgrade their investigating techniques and in the long run it was going to help them more than hurt them. And it had always been a common defense tactic, and a lot of cases were won on that blood-stained room in the police department and those pipes where they string them up and beat 'em and if I've heard it once I've heard it a hundred times – old criminal defense lawyers trying the whole case on the premise of the police having had him down in the back room and beating a confession out of him. Blind the jury to all the rest of the facts. Police brutality. Police did this. And win cases on just that kind of an argument. And that was already gone and I mean, you know, if they did what they were suppose to do no one could accuse them of that any longer. They would be required to go out and get the evidence. Dig it out, firm it up and really go to court with a case and not just that lousy confession that was always suspect. They go get the fingerprints, they do the scientific analysis, they do the ballistics, they do whatever was necessary to prove the case, absent the confession and if, in fact, they got a confession they were going to have one that was above reproach.

Stambler: So then confessions really became frosting on the cake.

Flynn: Exactly.

Wallenstein: Was that well received, did they buy that?

Flynn: Not for a long time.

Stambler: Depending on the age of the policeman.

Wallenstein: Well, I had two cousins who were policemen in New York, detectives, Brooklyn and I remember them coming to the house and they just wanted to tear the place apart. They had every conceivable scenario of how guys were going to walk away.

Flynn: Yeah, it was a long time.

Stambler: But I think the overview initially by the public, too, was the fact that how could these guys who had perpetrated a crime and everybody knew they did it and there was this and this and because they were not given the right, had not been read their rights, they were set free and I think that was the big thing that upset people the most. And I think it still upsets them today. Because you read about a case in the paper where, there was one very recently in Los Angeles, I don't know was it a robbery and shooting or something like that...

Flynn: It still happens, there have been some real brutal murders. I remember one happened right after Miranda.

Wallenstein: Yes, a Puerto Rican laborer, stabbed his wife and children.

Flynn: Yes, something and they had absolutely no evidence but his confession. The case was thrown out of there. They dismissed the case. There was a great hue and cry. The public still can't accept or understand, as you say, how can a patently guilty individual who has confessed get away simply for some technicality. And it is hard to understand. But it applies to everything. The Matt case, searches and seizures, line-up identifications, anything else, any of the constitutional requirements that result in someone's being set free. It's not something that's going to be accepted. They just can't recognize that it's as much for their protection as it is for the criminals' protection. They can't accept that.

Wallenstein: Well, it's kind of abstract. The other is one-on-one if you read the papers. You see some horrendous crime and you say to yourself, "How...?"

Stambler: Yeah. Where is the country going? That's the hue and cry.

Flynn: Boy, it really gets more complex than that. The ultra-conservative elements in our society are the ones who belabor these constitutional cases the most but they're the same people who want absolutely no governmental interference at any time in their lives. And it's an anomaly that you can't really put together. How could it be?

Stambler: It's amazing. If you talk to some of the Orange County conservatives, it just blows your mind. It's just exactly what you say, John. They want their cake and eat it too.

Flynn: They want it not to apply to them. But I don't think it created a lot of stress. It did in my personal life. I got involved in seminars and lectures, travelling all over the country trying to put together with the American Bar Association the code of Criminal Procedures, minimum justice standards. That's probably the ultimate product of Miranda in my view of what the case did. It jarred loose a recognition by the lawyers and the judges in the case that the criminal justice system in this country was in bad need of an overhaul. That it couldn't be done on an ad hoc, piecemeal basis by the Supreme Court. Somebody had to take hold. The American Bar Association created a committee delegated to the criminal justice section of the American Bar Association. A commission to draft a code of minimal standards in respect to the criminal justice system. We spent four years. prosecuting attorneys, defense counsels, judges, law school professors, Supreme Court set minimum standards. Then selling them across the country to the states. And it was an immense, tremendous project. And the outgrowth of it was just great. And that's why we now have, at least in this state, full discovery, full disclosure. Things like Miranda don't happen anymore. And cannot happen. It's no longer a game about who's gonna do this... it's now on the table. It has to be on the table; both sides know where they're at. All the rights are protected step by step. The system is much more efficient. It's still not perfect by any manner or means, but it is sure a hell of a lot fairer. And that resulted from Miranda. But this is a result of it: the Administration of Criminal Justice and the interesting aspect of it is that the first chairman of that committee was Warren Burger. Who is now the Chief Justice. So when you've got a case involving the application of one of those standards it's the best precedents that you can argue before the United States Supreme Court is that, uh, those rules. Then we were successful ... Arizona was the first state to adopt it.

Stambler: As it should have been.

Wallenstein: When I talk about stress, I'm trying to develop in my mind a sense...

Flynn: Only to the extent of my personal life. In relation to being asked to lecture at seminars, law schools, for conventions. Everybody wants to know about Miranda, the story of Miranda, how'd it happen and so forth and so on.

Wallenstein: You have kids?

Flynn: Yes. Two sets.

Stambler: You're a one-time loser.

Flynn: Yeah. I raised one bunch and I'm now raising another bunch.

Stambler: You know in the overview of the whole situation, again, based upon what you read and the reference material and what we were able to develop about you without even having met you and so forth, there are a lot of presumptions that we made in terms of the effect of the case on you. So far we have heard none of it. That's why we were hoping, you know we were reaching out for a little bit more only for a dramatic beat. When you said stress on your personal life. I mean was there pressure, peer group pressure? Was there pressure from family? Was it like why are you getting involved in this or was it...?

Flynn: Obviously, because of the notoriety created by Miranda, you're in demand to go to law schools, other bar conventions, other states, national conventions and to tell them about Miranda. And that takes you away from home for a long time. And you get caught up in the whirlpool of this kind of thing. I can remember flying on F. Lee Bailey's jet, parties, the whole thing. And then you get involved in cases away from home. A number of large cases in Colorado and California, Philadelphia. That creates a great strain on your personal life. In your office, jumping on a plane, going off for two weeks to try a case, coming back and there's no question in my mind that it was certainly responsible for one of my divorces. Not that the whole practice of law for a trial lawyer isn't a special situation. It's a tough, tough life. It's not really a satisfying experience for one's family. That's why I tried to cut back because I had to get... I wanted to spend time with my family. They're at the age when they need me. I've been to the pit enough times. I don't need to climb anymore mountains, achieve anymore successes. I do what I do economically because I want to pay for my farm and raise my family. But, uh, it deprived my kids of a lot of my life. It had to be a terrible strain on my wives. Day in and day out, the practice of law. You're in the court room from nine to five. But you're going to work that many hours on the outside if you're a good lawyer. Read every scrap. You've got to turn it in your mind. Your mind is enveloped and calculating and thinking and scheming for the next day's cross examination. And you go home and you're not fit for anybody … really. Then when it's all over there's that tremendous let down and relaxation. The idea is just to get drunker than hell to spin-off, chase women or whatever the hell you do. You get caught up in the whirlpool of travelling all across the country and all of the rest of it and that creates more stress and more strain, plus the lawsuits. You're more in demand. The cases get bigger, the responsibilities get heavier.

Stambler: The less time you're home for getting together with your…

Flynn: Exactly. It's like being caught up in a great big whirlpool going around on a treadmill, spinning faster and faster.

Wallenstein: And yet that is what you do. How can you avoid it?

Flynn: Oh you thrive on the courtroom. I mean, you know, it's like…

Stambler: Like an actor on first night.

Flynn: Well, sure it's like an athlete. That game. You don't want to quit. Keep going back, going back. Every case is different. Every case presents a new challenge. You end up being an expert in everything. One case may involve pubic hair. You'll read fifty books how you scientifically analyze, so you know more than that police expert does. You've got to or you can't examine him properly. I just finished a case, I never found out so much about pubic hair and I found out incidentally that it is absolutely the most unscientific basis upon which to try a case. There is no one capable or qualified at all yet – they've got men sitting in prison as a consequence of identifications based on pubic hair. When you get right down to it they cannot positively say that something is human or animal. They cannot determine sex, all kinds of things. People never pay any attention to it. They don't dig into it, they just accept. An expert gets up there and says, "in all my training, in my opinion they (the hair) are from the same source." And lawyers never ask him another question. It's just not so. There are a lot of things that a sophisticated examiner can do with a pubic hair. Cut it, section it, measure the core, scale count it, do all kinds of things with it. And if he does all of those things that are available to him by way of identification the best that he can say is that they are similar. That's all he can say. And the case I had, I had the expert and I said, "Now, did you do all of these things?" "No." "Based on the color and texture, whatever texture that there is you are not suggesting that this jury accept beyond a reasonable doubt that these two hairs came from the same source, are you?" "Oh, no I wouldn't want to do that." "Well, what the hell's the value of your testimony?"

Wallenstein: Forgive me for pursuing this, but is this your third marriage?

Flynn: Fifth.

Wallenstein: Fifth? My gosh.

Stambler: Forgive me for coming back to this, again, but in your taking on the Miranda case and it being a rape, robbery, kidnap case, was there any peer group pressure, did you belong to a country club? Did anyone say to you, "Why are you doing this, John?"

Flynn: No, not in any of that sense of the word. But, you've got to understand this in the context, I am now at that time a member of the largest law firm in Phoenix. Typical white collar, big, corporate, tax specialists, all aspects of a major law firm. We were representing indigent defendants for no fees. Corporate clients were paying ... you know. At the same time I was representing Westinghouse in a big products liability case. And I'm representing a criminal for rape, robbery, kidnapping. That's hardly conducive to associating with the general counsel for Westinghouse.

Stambler: That's exactly the question.

Flynn: And what kind of an image am I going to have when their case, when I'm in court, in front of a jury representing Westinghouse. To their everlasting credit the two major partners, the two senior partners Louis and Rocha did press ahead. It probably cost that law firm $20,000 for us to prepare that case. We got first class treatment on it. There wasn't a cut. There wasn't a case ever recorded in the history of the United States on confessions that wasn't pulled, copied, read, re-read, re-read and re-read. I can't begin to tell you the man hours that it took. Three of us went to Washington and all of that expense and all the rest of it, it had to cost them $20,000. And then representing in two trials, both of which lasted more than a week. By the way there is an interesting twist to the case that you ought to know about. And not ever was there a suggestion from the law firm...

Stambler: What about from the clients?

Flynn: A fellow by the name of Lyle Meyers was Vice President and General Counsel of Westinghouse Electric Company. Following Miranda, one or two years following it, I was invited to be the principal speaker at the National Association of General Counsels of America. There was the General Counsel of every major corporation in the United States. Ford, General Motors, all of them. Four or five hundred of them. It was with pride that he introduced me as Westinghouse's attorney and Miranda's. So the bottom line was that really big people accept that as a lawyer's responsibility and obligation. You can wear two hats. You can be just as good a lawyer for Westinghouse as you can defending Miranda in a trial of law.

Wallenstein: Yeah, from their point of view, hey, you're the guy.

Flynn: So I don't recall, in answer to your ultimate question, any pressure. More respect. A lot of lesser lawyers – but then I guess that's typical of society, how they view things, there may have been some resentment. We lost some civil cases but that's not borne out of any real thought. Now, the interesting twist that you ought to have as part of this whole picture occurred in the two cases. He's convicted and got 20-30 and 20-40 to run consecutively. There stacked one on the end of the other. He'll be in prison forever. We come back and a new case is set for trial and about that time I get a letter from Ernesto. He says, "What about my other case"? What about his other case? We hadn't taken revue to the United States Supreme Court for his other case even though it was based on a second confession which was an outgrowth of having already confessed. Now they're saying to him "Well, c'mon now Ernest, you've already confessed to this, give us the rest." The week following Miranda, the Supreme Court handed down a case, *Johnson vs. Hearst*, and that case held that Miranda was not retroactive, only prospective. Therefore, Miranda's case isn't going to help Miranda. And then we goofed, I mean we really goofed. In the enchantment over the first case we totally overlooked the second. We hadn't taken it up. Well, fortunately the old traditional rule is that if a confession is truly involuntary, i.e. the rubber hose or pipe, it was excluded under old involuntary traditional grounds. So we filed a writ of habeas corpus. First we asked for a hearing. The court set a revue and established that the second confession had been following the first confession induced by his first confession on the basis of a promise that, "You might as well tell us, you confessed to this. If not we'll give you worse on the second one." Which would be truly involuntary under old traditional standards. Our Supreme Court took a second look. "Hell, no." They were burned by Miranda. They weren't going to help Miranda. "Hell no." He stays there, 20-40. So we took Federal Habeas Corpus. And fortunately the Federal District Judge agreed that the second one was involuntary under traditional standards and granted the writ habeas corpus forcing the State to give him a trial –on the other one. It was a classical goof. Here's Miranda in court and "Miranda" can't even help Miranda.

Wallenstein: You look very athletic. Do you work out or is it just working on the farm?

Flynn: It's working on the farm. I do a little running in the morning. Basically it's building fences, irrigating and cutting wood.

Stambler: How far from here is your farm?

Flynn: About twenty-five miles. It's about a half-hour out there on the freeway.

Wallenstein: You know you mentioned that your area was police procedure. According to my research, the fellows who arrested Miranda were Carroll Cooley and Bill Young, Wilfred Young. Carroll Cooley went on to be a Police Captain, did he not? Is he still active? Or did he retire?

Flynn: No, he's still active. In fact, saw him last week. Came out to the house and borrowed the Miranda transcripts.

Wallenstein: Did you have much contact with him after that (the Miranda case)? You must have known him. Cooley, I'm talking about.

Flynn: Oh yeah, I know him. I knew who he was. Obviously, because of the case we became better acquainted through the trial and all the rest of it. He taught a class at the college on criminal proceedings. He still doesn't agree with the decision. He totally disagrees.

Wallenstein: Did he (Carroll Cooley) ever feel that he personally was under the gun because he and Bill Young were the arresting officers?

Flynn: No, I don't think so. He didn't take it on a personal basis. He was just doing what he had done all along. That's what criminal procedures were at that time. It was nothing out of the ordinary.

Stambler: An interesting aspect of this, and I think it needs to be brought out in the dramatization, is that the police were not doing anything wrong. They were not doing anything wrong.

Wallenstein: What were your feelings like as you came to know Miranda?

Flynn: Well, I liked him. He got caught up in the whole thing, as well. He came to recognize that the name Miranda was going to be something and it probably led to his downfall. Ultimately. He was not particularly articulate. He was a rather befuddled, knock-around, not a whole lot of education, in and out of jail and that sort of thing. As this thing began to emerge, he began to read. I got a couple of letters from him afterwards that were just really tremendous. Proud of his name, proud of what it stood for and all the rest of it. I kept them. Poignant. It was an insight into the impact of "Miranda" on [Emits Miranda] and it tells you what it meant to him. Then, in fact, when the second trial for rape and kidnapping he was convicted a second time. The judge was running the sentences together. He got credit for all the time and the sentences had been stacked. Second judge ran the sentences together so that it was all coming off the top and he was out in a short time. He came down off the bench and shook his hand. After the trial, after he was convicted. But he really wasn't sentencing him to anything. He just took the sentence and laid it on top of the other one so that it had no significance at all. It was like saying I'm not going to give you any more time. He had gotten down off the bench and shook his hand and that really meant something to him.

So now, he gets out. Immediately after his release, I saw him and talked to him. He had big plans. He was working as a draftsman in an engineering firm. Had something, really. And then he began to change because I think somehow he felt that the public would be waiting for him. He was a celebrity. There would be some kind of recognition and just nothing was happening. I mean, there was just nothing going on. There was no action for Ernesto Miranda.

Stambler: That has to be a rather frustrating thing to think of yourself as some kind of celebrity and the outside world still thinks of you as a heavy.

Flynn: Exactly. I don't have any confirmation of this, but I think it's true. Some of the police officers saw him. He was actually selling autographed cards with the Miranda warning on them. And then he left that job (draftsman) and I would see him once in a while, he would drop into the office and I could notice a more sullen… subtle change going. Next thing I know he got arrested out here. He had been carrying a concealed weapon; marijuana. We tried to help him but he was starting to become like he originally had been, sullen. Then, big problem came up. He ran into his ex-wife and daughter in a store. He wanted to talk to his daughter; she wouldn't let him.

Wallenstein: Was that his common-law wife?

Flynn: Twila. That was Twila.

Stambler: This was the daughter he threatened to take back?

Flynn: Now he comes down and he wants to see his daughter. So I said I'll write a letter for you but you've got to understand just how hard this is going to be. First, you've got to file a suit to establish paternity. Once you establish that you are the father then you've got to go to court and it's long and full of problems, but I'll write him a letter. I wrote a letter and I got a letter from the prosecuting attorney. She considered my letter as a threat and, you know, all hell was gonna break loose. I talked to him again. "Decide what you want me to do, I'm prepared to move forward." That was the last time I ever saw him. Just after that he was killed. But you could just see, you know, Miranda takes him way up here, articulate and lost.

Stambler: And that's the incredible dramatic twist in terms of the man.

Wallenstein: Explain something that has always been missing in my mind and that is why... It was 2:00 am in New York that Saturday night, the night he got killed and I just bolted up and I just couldn't believe it, I didn't know why. It just seemed so incredible. It was that he should have died that way. Now I read the paper accounts and at least according to the paper he was selling cards and he goes into this bar and he's playing poker and he ends up in a fight and I say to myself that seems to come out of left field. The guy has adjusted. He's been out 10 years or 6 years.

Flynn: That was the depression. And that's the coming down. And right back where he… If it hadn't been that it would have been something else, and probably back in prison.

Wallenstein: And Twila Hoffman? I have absolutely no sense of her at all. Wasn't it sort of a strange relationship?

Flynn: No, not really. Fit the pattern. She was not a quick person. She was sort of compatible. You could understand the relationship.

Wallenstein: You know, it occurs to me with the girl, Patricia Ann Weir, that it must have taken more than just a little bit of courage in those days to proceed with a rape case as the victim and the second time.

Flynn: I don't think so much the first time and again I don't think, Patricia left to her own decision would have. But I think it was her family, her in-laws and the prosecutors. Certainly the second time, pushing her.

Wallenstein: Was she married? Oh, it's her sister's in-laws.

Flynn: It was her sister's in-laws. Her brother-in-law mainly.

Wallenstein: They weren't afraid of her name being in the press?

Flynn: Apparently not and I don't think at that point the prosecutors would have let her, they subpoenaed her, they made her come to court, simple as that. The case was now more than just an ordinary rape case where the victim could say, "Hey, I don't want to go through this. I don't want to do it" and the prosecutors say, "I'll respect your feelings, forget it." It was way past that. It's Miranda now.

Wallenstein: That was the second time?

Flynn: That's the second time.

Wallenstein: The first time they had his confession. They just needed her…

Flynn: To identify him.

Wallenstein: So her family had no idea it would get so large. It was just open and shut.

Stambler: You said before you weren't particularly surprised. How did you hear about him (Miranda) getting killed?

Flynn: I guess, I heard it on the radio.

Wallenstein: Did you feel like you lost someone close to you? I guess you must.

Flynn: Yeah, I felt very bad about it. I just didn't see any reason the guy should end up like that. But I had seen his decline. That kind of thing could happen didn't surprise me.

Wallenstein: Tell me at any point that we're treading on too personal grounds. Would you give us the names of your kids?

Flynn: All of them?

Wallenstein: How many are there?

Flynn: Seven.

Wallenstein: What is their age range?

Flynn: 32 to 8. See those two on the end (points to picture) are mine, the other two are my step-children. There are five others.

165

Wallenstein: What's your wife's name?

Flynn: Cathy. The names are Mary, she's my youngest, age 10 and my earlier family, the older ones are Terry, 24...

Wallenstein: Any of them going to be lawyers?

Flynn: No. Michael is 26, Kathy is 28, John is 30 and Patricia is 32.

Stambler: So at least there is a John.

Flynn: I've got four grandchildren; about to have the fifth.

Wallenstein: Can I get the Miranda transcripts to have or to duplicate?

Flynn: Sure, as long as you promise to give them back. I might be able to dig out that letter for you. You might want it.

Wallenstein: How was he on the inside? Did he adjust (in prison)?

Flynn: He had no problem. He was a model prisoner. That's why he was released first eligible time.

Wallenstein: My research on him indicates that he was arrested twice for armed robbery in L.A., he had been thrown out of the Army as a peeping tom and there was this incredible thing about walking by a house one day, sees the door is open and walking in and getting into bed with some woman, which takes more than a little guts. You've got to be by my conservative estimate a little crazy.

Flynn: I expect that while all of this was happening he had a drinking problem of some severity and that the decline started afterwards, when he took up the drinking again. When he was caught with a small amount of marijuana, concealed weapon he had been drinking. He was at the bar drinking when the stabbing happened. I think that the underlying drinking problem of some severity and that's what caused all of his earlier difficulties and then when he was in prison he didn't drink, came out, everything was great, got a job, was on a high but doesn't get the notoriety, frustration, starts drinking again.

Wallenstein: Sees his wife.

Stambler: You say he was working as a draftsman when he first came out? It was a trade he picked up in prison?

Flynn: Apparently so.

Wallenstein: So prison actually benefitted him in that he couldn't drink...

Stambler: He obviously became a little more articulate.

Wallenstein: As he got some self-esteem. Why did she (Twila) begrudge him (Miranda)?

Flynn: Well, in the migration of things the threat in prison – if I get out I'm going to take that girl away from you. That started it. Now she has gone to court and helped get him convicted and back in prison. If he was mad before, what's their relationship now? You know, she never wants to see him out of that prison. I'm sure it was a terror in her life that he was on the street walking around some place.

Stambler: Well, he didn't make a bee-line to find her, running into her was just coincidence.

Wallenstein: She still live relatively in the neighborhood?

Flynn: Apparently in Mesa somewhere.

Wallenstein: His Dad was a painter in Mesa so I guess he just drifted back there. Their daughter would be about 16 or 17 by now.

Stambler: Then he really had no family at all.

Flynn: Sister, mother, brother.

Stambler: Are they still alive?

Flynn: As far as I know. I've never met them or talked to them. They never manifested any interest.

Wallenstein: Do you think Carroll Cooley would talk to us?

Flynn: I think so, he's a real nice easy-going guy.

Wallenstein: You know, I called over (to the Phoenix police) – oddly enough the fellows accused of killing Miranda, they said they thought were in Brownsville. That they're still wanted on open warrants. They felt that they went back and forth across the border. Every now and then they heard they were still at large. I got the impression that they didn't really turn themselves inside out to get these guys.

Flynn: I didn't get that impression either.

Wallenstein: Once they were out of the jurisdiction, you know, and I'm wondering if there isn't some lingering resentment even though it was explained and they appreciate it brought them into the 20th Century.

Flynn: Well, they got the one guy

Wallenstein: Yeah, but they let him go.

Flynn: Yeah, well they didn't have any evidence.

Stambler: Even though he was identified by the gal in the bar.

Flynn: Yeah, they made a lot out of "Miranda" – didn't help Miranda. Local cartoonist did a cartoon on the editorial page. A gallows. No appeal. "Miranda" doesn't help Miranda. "Sorry, Ernie, no appeal."

Wallenstein: Ooomph. A little heavy-handed wasn't it?

Flynn: But that was the sentiment.

Stambler: That was really the question we were asking earlier.

Flynn: Yeah, okay, you know this is really a conservative community in many respects. Law and order is the order of the day. Technicalities in the law. Justice is not only blind, it staggers. The local press was totally dominated by the Phoenix newspapers, which were very conservative.

Wallenstein: Did they ever turn any of that on you?

Flynn: Oh yeah. I've been in and out of the papers for a long time.

Wallenstein: You say that with a smile – but I'm betting there's a lot of water under that bridge.

Flynn: Oh, you bet.

* * *

APPENDIX B

PETITION TO THE UNITED STATES SUPREME COURT

RECEIVED

JUL 16 1965

OFFICE OF THE CLERK
SUPREME COURT, U.S.

IN THE

SUPREME COURT OF THE UNITED STATES

OCT. Term, 1965

~~No. 1994.~~

No. 419 Misc.

ERNESTO A. MIRANDA, Petitioner,

v.

STATE OF ARIZONA, Respondent.

PETITION FOR WRIT OF CERTIORARI TO THE
SUPREME COURT OF ARIZONA

John P. Frank
John J. Flynn
Phoenix Title &
Trust Bldg., 9th flr.
Phoenix, Arizona 85003

TABLE OF CASES (Cont'd.)

IN THE

SUPREME COURT OF THE UNITED STATES

_____ Term, 1965

No.

ERNESTO A. MIRANDA, Petitioner,

v.

THE STATE OF ARIZONA, Respondent.

_____

PETITION FOR WRIT OF CERTIORARI TO THE

SUPREME COURT OF ARIZONA

Petitioner prays that a Writ of Certiorari issue to review a judgment of the Supreme Court of Arizona of April 22, 1965, which became final on May 7, 1965, by virtue of the failure of previous court appointed counsel to file a petition for rehearing within fifteen days as required by Rule 9 of the Rules of the Supreme Court of Arizona.

OPINION

The opinion of the court below is reported at 401 P.2d 721. A companion case affirming the conviction of the defendant for robbery is reported at 401 P.2d 716.

JURISDICTION

The judgment of the court below was entered as noted above, on April 22, 1965, and became final on May 7, 1965. The time to move for a rehearing under the rules of the Supreme Court of Arizona had already expired by the time present counsel was requested by the American Civil Liberties Union and the petitioner to examine the case for possible error. The case itself is an appeal to the court below in a criminal case. The defendant has been sentenced to imprisonment for the crime of kidnapping (Count I) for from twenty to thirty years and for the crime of rape (Count II) for from twenty to thirty years, the sentences to run concurrently. This Court has jurisdiction to review the Supreme Court of Arizona under 28 U.S.C. Sec. 1257 (3).

QUESTION PRESENTED

Whether the written or oral confession of a poorly educated, mentally abnormal, indigent defendant, taken while he is in police custody and without the assistance of counsel, which was not requested, can be admitted into evidence over specific objection based on the absence of counsel?

CONSTITUTIONAL PROVISIONS INVOLVED

In all criminal prosecutions, the accused shall enjoy the right to a speedy and public trial, by an impartial jury of the State and district wherein the crime shall have been committed, which district shall have been previously ascertained by law, and to be informed of the nature and cause of the accusation; to be confronted with the witnesses

against him; to have compulsory process for obtaining
Witnesses in his favor, and to have the Assistance of Counsel
for his defence. (U.S.C.A. Const. amend VI)

Section 1. All persons born or naturalized in the
United States, and subject to the jurisdiction thereof, are
citizens of the United States and of the State wherein they
reside. No State shall make or enforce any law which shall
abridge the privileges or immunities of citizens of the
United States; nor shall any State deprive any person of
life, liberty, or property, without due process of law; nor
deny to any person within its jurisdiction the equal
protection of the laws. (U.S.C.A. Const. amend XIV, Sec. 1)

STATEMENT

Petitioner, a 23 year old indigent at the time of
the interrogation, was charged with the kidnapping and rape
of one Patricia Weir in Maricopa County (Phoenix), Arizona,
which allegedly occurred on March 3, 1963. On March 13, 1963,
for reasons never adduced at trial, defendant was apprehended
by Officers Cooley and Young at his home and taken to police
headquarters. (T. 44, 45, 55, 56) At the headquarters, the
petitioner was forced to stand in the "line-up" for possible
identification by the complaining witness in the present
case (T. 45) and for identification by the complaining
witness in the aforementioned companion case. Immediately
after this, the police took a confession from the defendant
without ever advising him of his right to counsel. Both
officers testified that the defendant was not advised of

174

his right to counsel. (T. 52, 53, 58, 59) At the subsequent
trial both the written confession (T. 53) and the officer's
recollection of petitioner's oral confession were received
in evidence. (T. 46-50, 57-58) Defense counsel specifically
objected to introduction of the written confession in the
following language:

> "We object [to introduction of the
> confession] because the Supreme Court
> of the United States says a man is
> entitled to an attorney at the time
> of his arrest." (T. 52-53)

The confession was admitted despite the specific objection,
and despite the fact that there had been no determination
as to the voluntariness of the confession which uses
language inconsistent with the petitioner's education.

On appeal, admission of the confession and testimony
of the officers relating to it were assigned as error in
view of Spano v. New York, 360 U.S. 315, 79 S.Ct. 1202, 3 L.
Ed.2d 1265 (1959). (Assignment of Error No. 4, Appellant's
Opening Brief, p. 7.) The Supreme Court of Arizona declared
both Spano and the more recent Escobedo decision inapplicable.
Escobedo v. State of Illinois, 378 U.S. 478, 84 S.Ct. 1758,
12 L.Ed.2d 977 (1964). The Escobedo decision was fragmented
into five crucial conditions not all of which were deemed
present in the petitioner's case: (1) the inquiry must have
focused on the particular suspect; (2) the suspect must have
been taken into custody; (3) the police must have elicited
an incriminating statement; (4) the suspect must have
requested and been denied an opportunity to consult with his
lawyer; and (5) the police must not have warned the suspect
of his constitutional right to remain silent.

175

REASONS FOR GRANTING THE WRIT

1. The Supreme Court of Arizona has given the Escobedo decision such a narrow construction that, for all practical purposes, the protections of the Sixth Amendment are not available to those persons in police custody who most need its protection: persons so unaware of their rights or so intimidated that they do not request "the guiding hand of counsel" at this crucial stage in the proceedings. It must not be forgotten that the petitioner possessed only an eighth grade education, was an indigent, and had a history of mental disturbance. Yet, judging from the opinion, the court apparently concluded that the Sixth Amendment was not available to the defendant--who had been apprehended at his home and taken to police headquarters and placed in a line-up for possible identification by the complaining witness--because the inquiry had not focused with sufficient clarity upon the petitioner. The court reached this conclusion because the complaining witness might be mistaken.

> "We call attention to the fact that the crime committed in the instant case occurred in the night time, and that there is always a chance of a mistake in identity under such circumstances on account of the excitement of the complaining witness, and difficulty of identity at night." (401 P.2d at 730)

It defies common sense to hold that a man specifically apprehended and placed in a line-up for identification by a complaining witness is not being more than just investigated; however, and far more importantly, in the instant case there was no such mistake as hypothetically posed by the court, and the officers proceeded immediately after the line-up to interrogate the petitioner. (T. 45, 46) Surely at this

point, at the very latest, the investigation had become
accusatory: a classic confrontation between one man and
his interrogators. Apparently in focusing upon the hypothetical situation, the court completely overlooked the
right of the petitioner to have counsel at the interrogation
following the line-up.

It appears, however, that the primary reason the
court did not feel obligated to follow Escobedo was that
the petitioner failed to specifically ask for counsel; as
noted, he was not advised of his right to counsel. (T. 53,
58, 59) The court felt that by reason of previous arrests
"he [petitioner] was certainly not unfamiliar with legal
proceedings and his rights in court." (401 F.2d at 731)
This reasoning, often used in conjunction with the pernicious
waiver doctrine to deny the accused his constitutional
rights, always fails to account for the accused's failure,
if so experienced, to request legal assistance. The implicit
contention that the petitioner has waived known rights
openly conflicts with a realistic appraisal of the facts;
specific knowledge is being imputed to petitioner which, if
existent, undoubtedly he would have invoked to obtain legal
counsel. We submit that the facts demonstrate that the
petitioner was relatively inexperienced and incompetent.

The court's interpretation of the Escobedo decision
and its reasoning really assists those least in need of
counsel, for, if a person has enough awareness or presence
of mind to ask for counsel, he will be provided with the
same, or, if he isn't, any subsequent confessions will be
held inadmissible. However, if through fear or lack of

knowledge the accused fails to request an attorney, any
and all confessions wrung from him will be held admissible.
Surely, such a perversion of a constitutional doctrine can
not be tolerated; and, at least one distinguished federal
court has directly so held recently. U.S. ex rel. Russo v.
State of New Jersey, 345 F.2d ___ (3d Cir. May 20, 1965).
This Court has flatly declared that important constitutional
rights cannot be made to turn upon request; if applicable,
the constitutional safeguard must be recognized absent a
knowing and valid waiver. Carnley v. Cochran, 369 U.S. 506,
82 S.Ct. 884, 8 L.Ed.2d 70 (1962).

      2. In all fairness to the Supreme Court of Arizona,
it must be acknowledged that other jurisdictions, including
federal courts on occasion, have also distinguished the
Escobedo decision because the accused failed to specifically
request counsel. This, then, brings us to the second reason
why this petition should be granted: so that the current
widely conflicting treatment of a basic constitutional right
can be resolved and substantial and similar justice attained
by all accused persons wherever they live. The proper
interpretation of the right to counsel and the Escobedo
decision have been the source of controversy and litigation
in the state and federal courts. The grudging treatment
accorded the Sixth Amendment by the Supreme Court of Arizona
in the instant case, by the Maryland Court of Appeals in
Anderson v. State of Maryland, 237 Md. 45, 205 A.2d 281 (1964)
and by the Nevada Supreme Court in Bean v. State, 398 P.2d
251 (Nev. 1965) cannot be reconciled on factual distinctions

with the more liberal--and, we submit, the proper--treatment
accorded the Sixth Amendment and its implications as set
forth in Escobedo by the California, Rhode Island, Oregon,
Virginia and other courts in such cases as People v. Dorado,
42 Cal. Rptr. 169, 398 P.2d 361 (1965) appeal pending, 33 U.
S.L. Week 2415 (June 1, 1965) (No. 1012), State v. Dufour,
____ R.I. ____, 206 A.2d 82 (1965), State v. Neely, ____ Ore.
____, 395 P.2d 557 (1965), and Cooper v. Commonwealth, ____
Va. ____, 140 S.E.2d 688 (1965). This petition, therefore,
comes to the Court in much the same posture as petitions
alleging that the federal courts of appeals have decided the
question raised inconsistently. The questions raised by
this petition, and the diverse treatment they have received,
warrant, nay demand, that this petition be granted so that
the critical constitutional issue involved is finally
resolved.

CONCLUSION

There is little about the petitioner or the crime
for which he stands charged that commends itself. But the
cause of due process is ill-served when a disturbed, little-
educated indigent is sentenced to lengthy prison terms
largely on the basis of a confession which he gave without
being first advised of his right to counsel. This petition,
therefore, squarely raises the question of whether the right
to counsel turns upon request; whether, in other words, the
knowledgeable suspect will be given a constitutional
preference over those members of society most in need of
assistance. We respectfully ask that certiorari be granted

-8-

179

and the judgment of the court below be reversed. In view
of the fact that the <u>Escobedo</u> decision has been misapplied,
we would further ask the Court to reverse the judgment
summarily.

Respectfully submitted,

LEWIS ROCA SCOVILLE BEAUCHAMP & LINTON
Phoenix Title & Trust Building
Phoenix, Arizona 85003

By _____
        John P. Frank

and

_____
        John J. Flynn

July, 1965

-9-